Protected
ALLAN YASHIN

iUniverse, Inc.
Bloomington

Protected

This is a work of fiction. All of the characters, names, incidents, organizations, and dialogue in this novel are either the products of the author's imagination or are used fictitiously.

iUniverse books may be ordered through booksellers or by contacting:

iUniverse
1663 Liberty Drive
Bloomington, IN 47403
www.iuniverse.com
1-800-Authors (1-800-288-4677)

Because of the dynamic nature of the Internet, any web addresses or links contained in this book may have changed since publication and may no longer be valid. The views expressed in this work are solely those of the author and do not necessarily reflect the views of the publisher, and the publisher hereby disclaims any responsibility for them.

Any people depicted in stock imagery provided by Thinkstock are models, and such images are being used for illustrative purposes only.

Certain stock imagery © Thinkstock.

ISBN: 978-1-4502-9111-8 (sc)
ISBN: 978-1-4502-9113-2 (dj)
ISBN: 978-1-4502-9112-5 (ebook)

Printed in the United States of America

iUniverse rev. date: 02/11/2011

To JUDY....for all your love, patience and support and DANA....for your great ideas for the story

Prologue

The man stood in the doorway looking at his two young sons. Both were sitting on rocking horses he had just given them and making believe they were in a race. He smiled ruefully at their whoops of excitement, thinking of all the wonderful times he would be missing until he saw them again, the years of growing up he would miss until he came home again.

The boys looked up and saw their father in the doorway. They jumped off their horses and ran over to him. He grabbed both of them in his arms and swung them around so fast that their legs flew out behind them. They screamed with laughter and when he put them down they protested with shouts of "More, more!"

"That was so much fun, my boys! Now come, Cal and Pete, sit on your dad's lap. I've got something important to tell you." The boys quieted and stared into their father's eyes. Then he told them that there was a war going on far away and he was a chaplain and was going to go there to help the soldiers. Even at their young ages, the boys had been exposed to enough television to have some idea of what a war was. He told them that he would miss them very much but they didn't have to worry about him because he was going to be very careful. He would be thinking of them all the time he was away and he hoped they would think of him, too.

The last thing he said to them was, "I wish I didn't have to go, but it is our responsibility to help others when they need help the most. I want you boys to remember that."

Then the boys threw their arms around their father's neck and hugged him as tightly as they could. It was the last time Cal and Pete ever saw him, and so he never lived to see the day when his sons each had a rocking horse tattooed on his right hand in loving memory of the father they lost as young boys.

1

Chapter 1

THIRTY YEARS LATER

Of course, no one believed young Tommy when he told them he had been saved from drowning by his dead father, Cal. But Tommy insisted that was what really happened on the day he went to the park for a picnic with his mother.

Tommy and his mother Lucinda, often came to this park on the outskirts of Seattle. They packed Tommy's favorite peanut butter and grape jelly sandwiches that he had been eating for lunch every day for the past two school years. Lucinda brought yogurt for herself; since they lived a half hour drive from the park it was still cool by the time they started to eat. They spread their food out on Tommy's old bedspread that was now too small for the "grown-up" bed Tommy had graduated to when he turned nine this year. He still loved to look at the embroidered pictures of firemen and policemen going about their duties on his old bedspread.

Lucinda always responded warmly to the memories of Tommy telling her as a young child, "Mom, that's goina be me when I grow up. I wanna be helping people when they in trouble." Lucinda understood what it was like to be in trouble and then having no one who could really help. Maybe Tommy *would* make a difference in someone's life one day. Till then, he made a huge difference in *her* life.

After they finished their lunch, Lucinda would lean against a tree, reading a paperback mystery she had taken out from the library, while Tommy explored the banks of the stream that stretched alongside the picnic meadow. His science teacher had told the class that since it was the beginning of spring it would be a good time to look for tadpoles. Tommy had brought a net and a glass jar to the park and planned to bring the tadpoles he caught into school the next day.

But the stream was running fairly quickly and deep from the winter runoff and Tommy couldn't spot any tadpoles in the rushing water. He moved further and further downstream hoping to find something to catch with his net.

Lucinda was used to Tommy exploring the park so she didn't look up from her book. If she had, she would have noticed that Tommy had followed the stream deeper into the wooded area behind a thick growth of trees.

He walked bent over, peering into the stream until finally he spotted something. In the middle of the stream, protected by a near circle of large rocks, Tommy saw a pool of calmer water. Despite the shade caused by the overhanging branches, he thought he saw a school of tadpoles. He stepped out onto one of the rocks in the center of the stream, but the rock was slippery. As he tried to bring his other foot over onto the rock he fell into the water.

The water was far colder and deeper than Tommy would have imagined. He began to shiver as he reached out to grab hold of one of the rocks but the swift water started to carry him downstream. Tommy realized that he was in big trouble. His movements became more frantic as he splashed and turned towards shore hoping to be able to pull himself out. But his head smashed into a rock that jutted out of the stream and he started to go down. He couldn't keep his head above water and closed his eyes as he went under for the second time. Even as this was happening, Tommy thought of his mother reading under the tree and wondered if she would ever find him.

And then a hand with a rocking horse tattooed on it reached out for Tommy. He was grabbed by the collar and pulled gently out of the water and carried to the side of the stream. Tommy lay there panting, not thinking… just feeling the solid ground supporting him. He turned and looked up to see the face of the man who had saved him, just as his rescuer walked away and back into the woods.

Lucinda walked along the stream calling Tommy's name. When he didn't answer she broke into a run looking for signs of him on either side of the water. She found him standing at the side of the stream staring out toward the woods. As she got closer she realized that he was soaking wet. She dropped to one knee and turned Tommy so that she could look into his eyes. "My God, Tommy! What happened?"

The boy stared back at his mother. Despite what he had been through he was remarkably calm. "I was looking for tadpoles and I fell in the water. But I'm O.K. He saved me."

"Saved you! Who saved you?"

"It was Dad. Dad saved me."

"So, please sit down while I take a look at your file, Miss Benson. Hmm, so let me see, Lucinda. Is it alright if I call you Lucinda?"

"That's fine, Officer Washington."

"So, you put in a Missing-Person report on your husband, Cal, about two weeks ago."

"That's right, but he's not my husband. He's the father of my child, Tommy. We were living together until a year ago but we never got married."

"Not so unusual a story these days, is it, Lucinda? And he just disappeared one day?"

"Not exactly; we were having problems and we'd talked about the possibility of us separating for awhile."

"But you said that was a year ago. Why'd you wait till now to put in a Missing-Person?"

"It was better for us, Tommy and me, that he was gone. It all goes back to Cal's father. He was dead before I met Cal, but he gave Cal this notion that we're each responsible for helping other people when they're in trouble. That's a nice concept, but I always thought your biggest responsibility should be to your own family first. Cal seemed to have a lot of trouble living his life that way. Instead, he involved himself with a group of marginal-type people. Drugs were a big part of what was going on. He was trying to help them, said it was his *calling*, but things got out of control. When they started to use our house as a meeting place, with Tommy sleeping upstairs, well that was more than I could tolerate."

"I can understand you feeling that way. So what made you change your mind two weeks ago?"

"I saw Cal…I mean Tommy saw him… in the woods, down by the park. Tommy said he pulled him out of the water, maybe saved him from drowning. I guess he's still around. Maybe he does care about us. I'm worried about him. And I'm also scared that he's following us…I thought that it's time I let you try to find him and maybe he can get some help.."

"You did the right thing, Lucinda. But the trace on him just came back and whoever that was who helped your son in the park, it wasn't him. I'm sorry to be the one to tell you this, but our records show that Tommy's father died of an overdose six months ago."

Chapter 2

The wind was howling so fiercely that Reiko had to push against the front door of her home with all of the force in her small body in order to shove it open so that she could walk out into the swirling snow.

It was only six in the morning and still dark in the northern mountains of Japan, but Reiko needed to do one important chore before the school bus came to pick her up in an hour. The family cow, Mioshi, had acted strangely yesterday, refusing to leave the barn to graze, and Reiko wanted to see if she could find the reason. The cow was too old to produce much milk and Reiko knew that her mother only kept the Mioshi because Reiko had always been attached to it. And now, Reiko was the only one in the family who could approach the cow without fear of being butted or kicked.

Reiko trudged over the path that led to the wooden barn 100 feet away from her home. Now that she was nine years old she was strong enough to lift up the heavy log that kept the barn door closed. She closed the door behind her and even though it was still dark in the barn, she managed to see the cow standing in her stall.

Mioshi mooed when she saw Reiko and came to the front of the stall to have her head rubbed. When Reiko saw the cow was limping she decided that she would have to get a good look at the cow's foot. She retrieved the oil lantern always kept in the corner of the barn, lit it, and walked into the stall.

Normally, Reiko's father or older brother would have been there to help her, but early this morning they had left from their farm on the outskirts of Kasagi to drive their old truck to the farmers market in Kyoto to sell their crop of snow cabbage, and they wouldn't be back until later that day. So Reiko carefully put the lantern on the floor of the stall and walked closer to her cow.

Reiko made the kind of cooing noises you might normally make to a young baby and gently rubbed the cow's head and patted her flanks.

Reiko bent down and slowly lifted the cow's left rear leg and saw what was causing the problem. In the light from the lantern she was able to see a large nail protruding from the bottom of the hoof. Reiko had seen her father remove similar things from the cow on many occasions, so she knew just what to do. She went to the tool box kept in the barn and selected the pair of pliers her father used. She went back to the stall and again gently lifted the cow's leg until she could see the nail. The cow mooed but let Reiko do what was necessary.

Reiko got a grip on the nail with the pliers but when she tugged she realized the nail was embedded more deeply that she had thought. Reiko took a tighter grip on the pliers and yanked on the nail as hard as she could. The nail came free, but Mioshi bellowed in pain and kicked back with her leg. Reiko was knocked backward and landed on the lantern. She quickly got to her feet but in seconds the straw in the stall was ablaze. Almost instantly, the fire spread to the rest of the barn. The flames climbed upward as they consumed the old wooden framework of the barn.

Reiko wouldn't leave the burning barn without Mioshi, but thick smoke was filling the barn and she was unable to pull the frenzied cow from her stall. Reiko finally decided that she couldn't save her cow but had to get out of the barn herself.

But the path to the door was blocked by a wall of flames. She ran towards a window but a wooden beam from the ceiling crashed to the floor and she couldn't get through. She started to cough and gag as the smoke filled her lungs. She remembered that in a fire the fresher air was always at the bottom so she lay down on a patch of ground that wasn't on fire yet. The heat and smoke burned her eyes, she closed them and lay there listening to the sounds of the fire crackling and roaring around her and the wild mooing of her cow as it ran back and forth in the stall.

As the air filled with smoke Reiko tried to hold her breath as long as she could, but each time she was forced to inhale she took in more and more smoke, her nostrils burning from the heat of the air. Even though her eyes were closed her head started to swim. She strained to remain conscious despite the intense heat surrounding her. She heard Mioshi collapse on the ground near her. And then in a few seconds she felt and heard nothing at all.

Reiko's father saw the smoke in the sky as he rounded the last bend in the road leading to his farm. He pushed his old truck to its maximum speed and jumped to the ground as soon as he reached his driveway. His son was already crying as he ran after his father to the barn. They found Reiko's mother kneeling in the snow, her head in her hands, sobbing. The barn had collapsed in on itself, a wreck of smoldering wood. Reiko's father stared at what once had been his barn. Then he placed his hand on his wife's shoulder. Trying to comfort her, he told her that the barn was old anyway. It was time for a new one.

She didn't look up at him, but only pointed towards the barn and said one word, "Reiko!" Reiko's father charged into the smoke-filled barn, calling Reiko's name as he pushed his way past the barn's wooden supports now lying at odd angles on the blackened floor. He saw nothing but burned wood and random patches of still-burning hay.

He feverishly searched for any sign of Reiko and then noticed a charred mound in a corner where the stall once had been. He stepped over fallen beams and approached the body of Reiko's cow. Reiko's father had difficulty breathing in the smoke-filled air, he stopped to put his hands on his knees and lower his head. Then he saw Reiko's foot sticking out from under the cow's body. Shoving with all his strength, he managed to roll the Mioshi over and there he saw his daughter lying on the burned straw.

Reiko's father gently picked up her limp body and carried her out into the cold morning air. He was not the type of person who gave himself permission to give in to his emotions, but as he carried Reiko's body over to his wife and son, tears filled the creases in his weathered face.

And then Reiko opened her eyes and gasped for air. She hugged her father tightly and, between coughs, managed to say, "Mioshi, Mioshi, where is she?"

Five minutes later, Reiko's breathing had returned to normal and as her mother gently washed the soot from her face, she looked beseechingly at her father. "Please let me see Mioshi, father. I must help her."

"I wish I could tell you something different, my daughter, but your cow has perished in the fire. It is too late for her."

"Then let me say goodbye to my cow, father. Please let me do that!"

Reluctantly, Reiko's father carefully led her back through the smoldering ruins of the barn. When they reached Mioshi's body, Reiko's father placed his arm on her slender shoulder. "See, her body is still. The lungs are filled with smoke. There is nothing that can be done."

Reiko knelt down and petted Mioshi's head. She leaned over and kissed the cow on its forehead, then stood and took her father's hand and they began to walk out of the barn. But then they heard a noise behind them and they turned to see Mioshi's tail thumping back and forth against the burned hay. A moment later she struggled to her feet and then slowly walked over to Reiko and pressed her big head against Reiko's chest.

Chapter 3

Sandor had to take his little brother Billy with him whenever he went out to play. He hated having to do this. He stood in the doorway of his home and complained to his mother, "I'm nine years old. None of the other kids my age have to drag along their little brother when they go out."

"Don't tell me about the other kids. It's ok with *their moms* if they sit home and stare at the tube all day. Not me! If you're going out in the fresh air to have fun, Billy's going along too. So, if you're not taking him with you, get your rear end in here and close that door."

Sandor grabbed his little brother's hand, pulled him out the front door, and started the mile walk to the park. Hiding the hurt that he felt because his big brother hated to go out with him, Billy started to taunt Sandor, "Mommy made you take me. Mommy made you take me!"

Sandor squeezed his brother's hand until Billy winced in pain. "Shut up, you little jerk, or I'll leave you out here!"

"You can't leave me. I'm only four years old. You be in big trouble if you leave me."

They walked in silence for a while, Sandor mulling over all the injustices he had to endure at the hands of his mother. And as usual, his thoughts returned to an even bigger irritant than his little brother. It was his very *name*.

All the kids made fun of him.

"*Sandor*, who the hell ever heard of the name *Sandor?*"

"Here comes the sandy door."

"Get the vacuum cleaner; it's getting Sandor in here."

They were all so stupid, but he hated to hear them anyway.

Why couldn't his mother have given him an ordinary name, one that nobody would ever notice as being different? He looked at his brother and thought, "I get *Sandor* and she calls him Billy. Just how not fair is that!" And he gave his little brother's hand an extra-hard squeeze.

His mother always told him "You should be proud of the name Sandor. It was the name of your father's great-great-grandfather and he was a general during the Civil War." Sandor's mouth twisted in an ugly grimace as he thought to himself, "Who gives one big crap about the Civil War *or* my father! When the hell's the last time I saw him or he even called me? Like I bet he doesn't even know I'm nine years old already!"

Billy broke the silence between them by asking, "Are we get there soon? I'm tired of walking."

"Then you shoulda stayed home with your *Mom-my*. Come on! We'll be there in a coupla minutes."

The land was so flat in this part of Idaho that Sandor could see the park about a quarter of a mile off in the distance. The railroad tracks and a few ugly scrub trees were the only things that caught his eye as he looked across the windblown trail that led to the playground.

When Sandor finally walked into the park with Billy trudging behind him, he was greeted by the derisive remarks of the few kids there. "Here comes Sandman the baby sitter!".... "Hey, Sandbox, did your mom send your little brother to watch you in case you needed some help getting on the swings?"..."Hey Billy, next time come to the park by yourself and leave your loser of a brother at home!"

Sandor thought that if he ignored their catcalls they would eventually calm down and he could get into the game of tag they were choosing sides for. Scotty, the biggest boy in the group turned towards Sandor and said, "Wanna play? You can be on my side."

Sandor smiled and took a few steps forward, but then Scotty said, "I mean you, Billy. Nobody wants Sandor, the babysitter, on their side!"

Sandor grabbed Billy by the hand and rushed from the park. He hoped no one had seen the tears in his eyes.

As they walked back on the trail to their home, Billy complained "Why are we going? They wanted to play with me."

"Damn you! Shut your mouth...you've ruined enough for me!"

Sandor walked so quickly in his anger that Billy couldn't keep up with him. "Wait for me! You too fast! Don't go!"

Sandor reached the railroad tracks and turned to see that his brother was a hundred feet behind him and had stopped walking. Sandor saw that Billy was rubbing his eyes and crying. He was hollering something to him but Sandor couldn't hear because the 1:15 express train to Boise was coming down the tracks towards him. He angrily motioned and Billy started to walk over to him.

By the time Billy reached Sandor the express train was now roaring right behind them. The train made so much noise that Billy had to scream so that Sandor could hear him.

"I gonna tell Mommy that you left me…and you made me cry!"

Sandor's head started to throb as the sound of the train and his brother's screams bombarded him. "Now, you shut up right now, or you'll be sorry!"

"I not shuttin' up! Mommy's gonna punish you when we get home."

And as his brother taunted him, and the train rumbled and screeched past him, his head hurt so much he would have done anything to stop the noise.

Chapter 4

Lucinda was haunted by the thought of the mysterious man who saved Tommy. Who was he? Why did he just leave Tommy on the banks of the stream and walk off without waiting for someone to come for him? Was the man following Tommy as he walked along the stream or did he just happen to be there when Tommy fell into the water?

And the fact that Tommy said it was his father who saved him…was that the product of the imagination of a young boy at a time of extreme duress… the result of Tommy's wish that his father *could* be there to save him?

Or did the man actually *look* like Tommy's father? Lucinda knew that Cal had a brother, but she had never met him. Did he *resemble* Tommy's father? And if he did, would he have been following Tommy? Had he been asked to look after Tommy when his brother had been dying?

There were no answers to any of these questions.

On the infrequent occasions when she and Tommy went to the town lake or took long car trips to the nearest ocean beach, images of Tommy standing soaking wet at the side of the stream and talking of the mysterious man inevitably crept into her mind. But Lucinda eventually stopped trying to solve the mystery of that day. She just remained thankful to that man, whoever he was, for saving her Tommy.

As the years passed, Lucinda thought less and less of these things. She invested all of her energy into raising Tommy and, as all single moms do, took on the role of both mother *and* father. Her huge expenditure of time, patience, devotion and love were more than amply rewarded as Tommy grew into a fine young man.

Tommy was one of those rare boys who excelled in both academics *and* sports. He was the only boy in the history of his high school who put in a stint on the debating team and earned a letter at basketball at the same time.

When Tommy was a senior, offers of college scholarships appeared regularly in the mailbox. Lucinda knew that there were big things waiting for Tommy after he graduated.

And Tommy knew something too. All the years that had passed since that day his father saved him from drowning in the park, Tommy had known something. He knew that he was saved for a very special reason. He was saved by the man who could not possibly have saved him, and he was waiting to find out why. And when he did find out, he would be ready.

Tommy's grandfather had died years before Tommy was born, but he knew his grandfather had sacrificed his life serving as a chaplain, giving comfort to the soldiers in Viet Nam. Tommy remembered sitting on his father's lap as a little boy and listening as his father told him about his grandpa. "He was a brave and special man and he set an example of how all of us should live our lives. It's not an easy thing to do, but *I'm* trying and I know your grandpa would want you to try also."

When Tommy was eight years old his father left home one night and never returned. His mom tried to console him by telling him his dad loved him very much, but he had to leave to take care of some problems, and she hoped he would come back to them soon.

Yet Tommy always believed that his father had left because he had a special mission to perform, that it was his father's job to help those who were in trouble, that one day his father would return and tell him of all the good things he had done. Tommy waited, but his father didn't return. Not until the day he pulled his son out of that stream and saved him from drowning.

While Tommy was waiting for some outward sign of the path he was intended to take, he was developing his own belief system. He chose the debating team to test his conviction that people were creatures of reason. Despite the feelings, attitudes and prejudices one might bring to a situation, eventually pure, incontrovertible logic would become apparent, and all parties would be joined in agreement.

Underlying such a belief was Tommy's faith in the inherent goodness of people. He realized that to many people he seemed hopelessly naïve to say these things in the face of all the evidence to the contrary that one saw every day in the newspapers.

But Tommy believed that the harsh and even cruel circumstances of some people's lives bent and distorted the development of their souls, so they behaved in ways that were destructive to themselves and others.

And, yes, Tommy was also used to the disbelieving looks that came over faces when he mentioned the word *soul*. But, he was certain we all had one; certain that all our souls were waiting to be touched by the all- embracing force of the universe; a force above the divisiveness and destructiveness of commonly accepted religions.

Tommy was waiting for the time when he would be in a position to help someone, to change someone's life. And a month before he was to graduate high school he got that opportunity. He was about to get into his car after a late night basketball practice at the gym when he heard a voice behind him, "Hand over the keys to your car. I mean business!" Tommy spun around and saw a man standing in the shadows, wearing a baseball cap pulled low over his face. The man had his hand in his jacket pocket and seemed to be pointing a gun at Tommy.

"I don't wanna have to hurt you. Just give me the keys and your wallet. Do it now!"

Tommy felt no fear. He knew this was what he had been hoping for, the opportunity to take the same path as his grandfather and father. He held his hands up before him in a gesture of peace. Then he spoke in his calmest and most reassuring voice, "No matter how much you want my car and money right now, they are not the things that will bring you happiness. Accepting the universal force that binds us all together is the answer. Give me your trust; I can help you." And Tommy held out his hands to the man standing in the shadows.

Tommy was so late coming home from the gym that his mother was waiting for him on the porch. When she finally saw him walking up to the house she asked him, "Didn't you take the car tonight?" He didn't answer but then she noticed the big bruise on his forehead. "My God! What happened to you?"

Tommy shook his head and muttered, "I guess I'm not ready yet," as he walked past her and into the house.

Chapter 5

Whenever Reiko thought of the day of the burning barn she could recall only the image of flames and blackening smoke. Her father had spoken many times of how she had been miraculously protected but Reiko remembered nothing of that. She was not the type of child who dwelled on the past. Her focus was on the years ahead of her and what she needed to do to accomplish her goal. And what was her goal? Though she loved her parents greatly, Reiko needed to leave their small farm one day. She wanted to go to the far-off places she read about in books, wanted to go to a college where she would meet young men and women with experiences far different from hers.

As Reiko grew into her teenage years her great beauty caught the attention of many boys in her school. There was a stillness, a sense of inner directed strength and determined focus that added a veneer of mysterious unattainability that made her even more alluring.

But despite their efforts to attract her, Reiko resisted forming anything more than casual acquaintances with the boys who sought after her. She saw no good reason to form attachments here at home when she knew the future would take her to other, distant places.

A day hadn't passed since the burning of the barn that Reiko's father didn't fail to give thanks for the sparing of his daughter. Life had taught him that all people are but the servants of the gods, doing their bidding, and then either snuffed out too soon like a temple candle in a sudden storm or allowed to age until the wick no longer could support the flame of life.

But Reiko's father knew that something special had happened to his daughter. She should not have been able to endure the fire and smoke that day.

And he had been certain that the cow had been dead. No, there was a reason beyond his understanding to what had happened. And each day he prayed to the gods who preserved his daughter and hoped that they would eventually reveal their plans for Reiko.

Chapter 6

Sandor's mother knew there was something terribly wrong the moment she saw the expression on Sandor's face when he walked in the door without Billy. Her voice grew louder and louder, but he refused to answer any of her questions until she grabbed him by the shoulders with both hands and violently shook him. Then he silently turned and pointed out the door.

Sandor's mother ran out of the house and kept on running in the direction of the playground until she saw a group of people in the distance standing by the railroad tracks. She stopped running and sank down onto the dusty soil. She knew what they had found by the tracks.

Sandor's mother never believed his story about Billy's death. She knew that Billy might have had a fresh mouth for a four year old but he would never have tried to run home by himself. No, Sandor must have done something that caused his little brother to be hit by the train.

The town sheriff had his suspicions too, but Sandor held firm to his story. His brother was running home to tell his mother that Sandor had made him cry and he tripped and fell into the path of the train when he thought Sandor was going to hit him.

Sandor's mother threatened him, "I'm going to call your father and tell him what you did to Billy and then he's gonna come over and beat your ass till you're dead too!" But Sandor knew she really didn't want to see his father any more than he did. He'd be just as likely to beat *her* ass, as his.

The boys in the park treated Sandor differently after that day. They could sense that there was something changed about him, something about his expression and the way he stared them down when they tried to taunt him about what had happened to Billy. Now they let Sandor play with them. They didn't want to be his friend, but they felt it was safer to include him in their games than wonder where he was and what he might be thinking.

Sandor accepted their offers to be included in the group. He even enjoyed playing some of their dumb games at the park, but inwardly he thought they were pathetic, like chickens trying to make friends with the fox so they don't get eaten. Sandor knew that the chickens always get eaten.

Chapter 7

Reiko's father looked at the map he had taped to his bedroom wall. He stared at the line he had drawn in blue marker that stretched across the Pacific from Kasagi to Vancouver. He stared at that line every day and tried to imagine Reiko's new life. Then he closed his eyes and remembered how it came to be that his precious daughter was now so far from home.

He thought back to nearly two years ago, when Reiko was still living at home. His wife had become sick and he had to take her to the medical center in Kyoto. He rented a small room and each day walked the maze of city streets to reach the hospital to stay with his wife until she fell asleep each night.

The doctors didn't know when she would be well enough to go home, but as the days stretched into weeks it became clear that time would never come. Finally facing the eventuality that his wife would never return home again, Reiko's father told Reiko and her brother to come to Kyoto now, for this could be the last chance to see their mother before she was gone.

The next day, Reiko and her brother stood before their mother's hospital bed. She motioned for her son to come closer and she reached out for his hand. She told him he had been a good son to her and she prayed that she had been worthy of the task of raising him. And then as the words came harder, she said that she hoped he would wish to help his father and carry on the family farm. Reiko's brother told their mother that he would very much want to do this; as the tears welled up in his eyes, he kissed his mother one last time and then left the room, no longer able to bear the pain of seeing his mother slip away.

When Reiko approached the bed, Reiko's mother motioned for her husband to come closer so he might hear her voice that was now no louder than a whisper. "Promise to do this last thing for me. Reiko must go to my brother in Vancouver. He will give her the life she wants." As sad as it would make him to see his daughter leave, Reiko's father knew that she was right.

19

Reiko's destiny lay far away from home and he felt Vancouver was only the beginning of the journey.

Reiko's mother closed her eyes and her breathing became even shallower. A nurse entered the room and told them the effort to communicate with her family was exhausting Reiko's mother. It was time for her to sleep. After checking the vital signs on a monitor, the nurse informed them it would be safe for them to go home for the night and return the next morning. Then she drew the curtain around the bed and left the room.

Reiko's father moved the curtain slightly aside and softly kissed his wife goodnight. Then he took Reiko's hand and told her they would return early the next morning. But Reiko would not move away from the bed. "I'm not going home. I'm staying with my mother tonight. I need to be close to her one last time."

Reiko's father told her this was against hospital rules. But when he saw the sadness in his daughter's face, he could not deny her wish. And in his heart, he knew, at this point, it could do his wife no further harm. So Reiko's father kissed her and quietly left his daughter sitting in the chair next to his wife's bed.

And a moment after her father left the room Reiko pulled aside the curtain and gently lay down in the bed next to her sleeping mother.

When Reiko's father returned to the hospital room the next morning, he found a team of doctors surrounding his wife's bed. He steadied himself to hear the worst, but when Reiko saw him enter the room she ran over to him and threw her arms around his neck. "Oh, Father, something wonderful has happened! Mother is so much better this morning. The doctors cannot explain it. They say it must be a miracle!"

And as Reiko's father looked at his wife sweetly smiling at him from her bed, he knew the reason for her recovery. The miracle was Reiko.

A week later when the entire family was reunited on the farm, Reiko's mother insisted that she still wanted her children to act on the wishes she had made on her hospital bed. And so, when Reiko completed her junior year in high school she left home to live with her wealthy uncle in Vancouver.

She had met him and his wife when they had traveled to Kasagi years earlier. He remained as she had remembered him, an imposing man who was far kinder and more generous than might be expected from his forbidding appearance.

Reiko had taken English throughout her schooling in Japan, so she felt at ease in her new high school in Vancouver. There were many students of Asian heritage in her classes but she associated with them in only the most casual manner. The boys who even dared to approach her typically presented themselves as supplicants at the altar of her beauty and intelligence, and she felt uncomfortable with this fawning. Besides, she dismissed the idea of entering into any relationship, as she knew that she intended to fulfill her dreams for the future and would soon leave all of this behind. She was a senior and in a matter of months she would set off for what she had always thought of as her place of destiny, California.

Reiko's high school counselor recognized Reiko's brilliance. After only a few months in Vancouver she had already surpassed the grades of most of the other students in the senior class. Reiko told her counselor that with her uncle's blessings, and his wealth, she had hoped to go to one of the wonderful and important universities in California. Her counselor responded that he could have been more helpful if she had wanted to go to a college in Canada where he had close relationships with many of the admissions officials, but considering her fairly recent transfer from Japan, and the lack of "contacts" with admissions officers in California, he was only able to obtain placement in one of the smaller colleges; but an excellent one, nonetheless. He told Reiko that if she enrolled there, after one year her grades would enable her to transfer to any university she pleased.

Two months after she graduated, Reiko thanked her uncle and his wife endlessly for their love and support, and she boarded a plane to begin her travel to San Jose' State University in California.

And in Kasagi, Reiko's father looked at the map on his wall and carefully drew a line stretching from Vancouver to San Jose. Then he fell to his knees before the small altar he had built in his room and prayed for the gods to show wisdom and compassion as his daughter continued on the journey they had planned for her.

And as he did this, Reiko was impatiently sitting on the plane that would take her to the beginning of her new life in California. The plane had landed in Seattle to pick up more passengers, who were now making their way down the aisle to find their assigned seats.

Reiko felt that each of the new arrivers was an annoyance until she saw the tall, handsome, blond young man in a basketball jacket struggling to walk up the aisle with his large bag. She saw him and at once knew that one day he would be very important in her life. The same inner voice that told her there was no need to become involved with any of the young men in Kasagi or Vancouver, now was telling her that she would share her future with this blond stranger.

As her body and mind became alert and she wondered just how they would meet, he came towards her seat and accidentally bumped her arm. She looked up at him and smiled. It had begun.

Chapter 8

Tommy helped his mother out of the taxi and then got his luggage from the trunk. He saw there was a long wait at the check-in line at the airport so he told Lucinda to wait for him at the food concession near his gate.

Tommy waved to a few familiar faces from his high school graduating class he spotted on line as he inched along, pulling his large trunk behind him and holding his carry-on bag in his other hand. Tommy towered over most of the other people on the line and, because he was wearing his school basketball jacket, people who were into sports stared at him and tried to decide if he "was anyone."

And while people were watching him, Tommy himself was carefully watching the other people at the airport. He was looking for his father.

He was sure he had seen glimpses of him several times since that day his father saved him from drowning. The first time was when he was on the stage accepting his diploma during his elementary school graduation and he saw his father standing in the back of the auditorium. Once he was a face in the crowd during a championship basketball game. Other times Tommy had seen him in the audience during debating team contests against other high schools.

And each time, Tommy ran out into the crowd to see him...but he was gone.

The first few times this happened, Tommy told his mother. At first she comforted Tommy, saying things like "Yes, it would be wonderful if your father could be here now to see you. He'd be so proud." But, eventually, as Tommy grew older, his mother became less patient with him. "Look, Tommy, you're getting too old to believe in this sort of thing. I know you hate to hear this, but your father's dead and no amount of wishful thinking is going to bring him back."

After that, Tommy kept the sightings of his father to himself.

But today, here in the airport, as he was about to leave for college, Tommy felt sure his father would be somewhere in the crowd of people. He would let Tommy glimpse his face one more time to let him know that he still watched over him, still protected him.

Yet, when Tommy finally had checked his luggage and walked to the food concession where his mother was waiting for him, he still had seen no sign of his father.

As he approached his mother he saw that she had a handkerchief in her hand. "You're not going to cry, now are you, Mom?"

"Of course, I'm going to cry, Tommy! I'm not going to see you again until Christmas."

"Christmas! No way! I'll be home for Thanksgiving. Remember you promised to bake me a sweet potato pie to take back to college?"

"Yes, I remember, but even Thanksgiving seems so far off. You've never lived away from home before. The house is going to seem so empty."

"I know how you feel, Mom. But this is what we both dreamed about, a full scholarship to Stanford. All the sacrifices you made so I could get to this point. And California is only a couple of hours away by plane. You could even come out to visit me and make a vacation out of it."

"That's just what you need, Tommy. To be seen walking around the campus with your mother. Those frat boys would never let you forget it. No, I'm going to miss you like crazy, but I'm so thrilled for you. I know this is only the beginning of very special things for you, my son. So get on that plane and at least remember to call your old mother every now and then."

Tommy joined the end of the line of passengers handing their tickets to the attendants. He shuffled along, dragging his overstuffed carry-on bag on the floor behind him. Just before he entered the corrugated tunnel that connected the terminal to his plane, he turned and waved to his mother. She placed her hand over her heart and smiled at her son, then watched him walk into the tunnel and out of her sight.

Tommy slowly edged his way towards his seat in the rear of the plane. Most of the overhead baggage compartments were nearly filled, but he noticed there was room for his bag in the compartment across from his seat. When he tried to shove his bag into the small remaining space he accidentally bumped into the passenger sitting on the aisle.

Tommy instinctively said, "Excuse me. Sorry for that." And when he looked down at the passenger to apologize further he was greeted with a smile from one of the most beautiful girls he had ever seen.

Chapter 9

Reiko and Tommy sat across from each other on the aisle so they were able to talk throughout the flight. Each felt the same strong connection that seemed to go beyond pure physical attraction. Quickly getting past the superficial details of Tommy's life in Seattle and Reiko's background in Kasagi and Vancouver, they happily realized that they both were heading to colleges in California.

Tommy joked that all he had to do was walk out Stanford's front gate, hitch a ride heading south on Highway 101 and he would be in San Jose in an hour. Reiko didn't say anything, but her smile made it clear that she was pleased by that thought.

A brief silence fell over them and in trying to keep the conversation alive, Tommy thought of a question that was used as a group icebreaker during parties in high school. "So, tell me, what's the most unusual thing that ever happened to you?"

Reiko paused, and then said, "My father would never forgive me for telling you this, but now I am in America and I wish to leave his superstitious ways behind me." So Reiko told Tommy about the day the barn burned down. "My father says it was the work of the gods that saved me from the flames and smoke. They have a special path for me to take. And that is why, he says, I was protected."

When Tommy heard Reiko's story he knew that he had to tell her that he, too, had been protected. Tommy had only shared this with a very few close friends and they either looked at him in disbelief or told him to stay off those drugs and laughed at him.

But when he told Reiko how he was saved from drowning by his father, who everyone insisted was dead, Reiko did not look away in disbelief and she did not laugh. Instead, she reached across the aisle and took his hand. They looked into each other's eyes and they knew they were fated to meet on this plane to California. And they held hands until the plane was nearly ready to land.

Chapter 10

When their plane landed in San Francisco, Tommy and Reiko faced the reality of separating. Tommy was leaving the plane here and taking a bus south to Stanford. Reiko was ticketed to fly through to the San Jose airport. They'd exchanged cell phone numbers but were having difficulty saying goodbye.

"I sure wish I had a ticket to fly down to San Jose with you, but I'm going to have to get off here. I can't believe we've only know each other for about two hours."

"I don't want you to go, Tommy. I want to be with you."

Reiko and Tommy stood and hugged, but the impatient coughs of the people waiting behind them forced them to back away from each other to clear the aisle.

Tommy reluctantly grabbed his bag and started to walk backwards down the aisle, waving to Reiko and holding an imaginary phone to his ear to indicate he would be calling her. And just as he reached the front of the plane, Reiko called out to him, "Tommy wait, I'm coming with you!"

Reiko swung her bag out of the overhead compartment and made her way to Tommy. When she reached him she clutched his hand and they ran off the plane together.

As they stood in the terminal, Reiko excitedly said, "I'll take the bus with you! You get off at Stanford and I'll stay on until it reaches San Jose! I'll call the airline later and tell them to hold my luggage for me at the San Jose airport."

"You're right. Both schools are right off 101, we can do that!"

And this time when they hugged they didn't let anyone interrupt them.

Chapter11

Tommy and Reiko strolled hand in hand through the airport terminal lost in their thoughts about the last few hours and wondering what the future would hold for them.

Then Tommy realized they had been meandering through the airport for nearly an hour. "The bus! We're going to miss it!"

They ran to the luggage carousel and saw that Tommy's bag was going around on a solitary circular trip. "Great! It's still here. Maybe we can catch the bus."

They hurriedly asked an attendant the location of the bus heading south on 101 and dashed out of the terminal into the pouring rain of a typical late summer night in San Francisco. It was nearly midnight and the wet airport roads glistened in the headlights of the taxies waiting to pick up fares.

They got to the bus as it was nearly finished loading. Tommy handed his ticket and a twenty dollar bill to Reiko. "Here, give the driver my ticket and buy one for yourself. I'm going to store our bags under the bus."

Reiko went in the front door of the bus, handed the driver Tommy's ticket and the money for her ticket, then walked to the back of the bus. She found two empty seats just over the area where Tommy was stowing their bags. She banged on the window and Tommy looked up and saw where they would be sitting. He slammed the large cover of the luggage compartment shut and ran through the rear door of the bus just as it was beginning to pull away.

Reiko was sitting on the aisle and moved aside so Tommy could squeeze past her to sit in the window seat. He pulled in his long legs to fit into the cramped space, and then Reiko put her head on his shoulder and closed her eyes. Tommy reached for her hand and stared out the window as the road rushed past his rain- streaked window. As wonderful images of the future he would spend with Reiko raced though his mind, Tommy never could have imagined what was about to happen.

Chapter 12

Sandor stood on the stage of his high school auditorium and spoke clearly into the microphone. "I want to thank all of you who voted for me and helped elect me senior class president. And to those of you out there who didn't support me, I'm going to devote this school year to making you sorry you didn't."

And with that vastly ambiguous pronouncement, Sandor held up his arms in a triumphant gesture and walked off the stage to cheers. He was greeted backstage by a small gathering of classmates whom he trusted enough to allow to be in his in-group of right hand men. They did his bidding and fed him information that he might consider useful in maintaining his control over the others in his graduating class. It offered them a sense of security to feel they were on *his* side and not considered as one of his enemies.

His classmates had voted for Sandor because he was a big, good looking guy who had made all the right promises about better food in the lunchroom, new equipment for the gym and a bigger and better prom this year. And he had a surprisingly high intelligence that impressed most of the mainly mediocre students in his school. But, maybe even more important, he had an intimidating physical presence that he wasn't afraid to take advantage of. They heard what had happened a couple of years ago to the last guy who had crossed Sandor and when Sandor returned to school from a three month stay in the juvenile correctional facility, he had been received with reverence. Maybe it wasn't such a bad thing, after all, if the president of your high school class were someone people are afraid to push around.

And he had his way at home too. Over the years, his mother slid deeper into the grip of the bottle. She rarely went out except to the local 24/7 convenience store when she needed more smokes or beer, and this only because Sandor was too young to buy those things for her. So Sandor basically raised himself. The shopping, meals, laundry, the cleaning, he took them all on as his responsibility.

He even took control of the family's finances by the time he was a teenager. He'd practiced his mother's scribbled signature until he was able to endorse her monthly public assistance payment and then write checks to cover the mortgage and electric bills. He put his mother on an allowance that left her with only enough money for her beer and cigarettes. He signed her signature to any papers coming home from school that required a parental response.

And rather than resist, Sandor's mother accepted all of this with equanimity. She was only too happy to let him take charge so she could be left to her television set and her alcohol- smeared reveries about what might have been. Maybe if her father hadn't beaten her so often when she was a kid, or if her mother had a few less boyfriends after her father walked out on them. Or if she had paid more attention in school, or if she'd only waited longer to have a kid and picked a far better man to have one with, then maybe things would've worked out differently for her. And then there were the times she counted the years to figure out how old Billy would have been by now and if his love could have saved her from what she'd become. Yes, there was far too much for her to remember and regret to have time to worry about what Sandor might be doing with his life.

But there *was* someone who was very involved with Sandor. Someone Sandor thought of as his prize and his consolation for all he had been through with his family...Jeanna, the most beautiful girl in the school, the star of all the high school plays. If being elected class president made him the king of the graduating class, then surely she was fit to be his queen, and he behaved accordingly. Despite the occasional display of his violent temper with the locals in town, he had always treated Jeanna as the treasure he considered her.

On the night of Sandor's election, he took Jeanna out to celebrate in their favorite restaurant in Boise, the Bo-Ho. It was near the capitol building and local politicians and newspaper reporters digging for something of interest to write about, usually filled the bar and most of the small dining room. As usual, Jeanna caused half the heads in the place to turn in her direction when she walked to their table. And as usual, Sandor stared down at the floor as he walked behind her, smothering his impulse to smash someone's face in for the way they stared at his girl.

After they were seated, Jeanna reached across the table to hold Sandor's hand. He looked at her face and smiled as he noticed the light from the candle on the small table bring out the blond highlights in her hair. He leaned across the table and gently stroked the side of her face.

"I'm the luckiest guy in here and everybody knows it."

"That's us, Sandy, the two luckiest people in Boise."

"Only Boise? I thought in all of Idaho!"

And they both laughed at the little joke and squeezed each other's hand a little tighter.

During dinner, the talk turned, as it inevitably did, to their plans for the future. Jeanna had already been accepted to the Drama School at UCLA and would be moving to California after graduation. Sandor didn't have the money to go to college full time, but his counselor told him it was pretty certain that he'd be admitted to the film studies department in the evening division as a non-matriculated student. Sandor would work during the days and, after classes, come home to Jeanna and the apartment they would share.

As the school year worked its way closer to the end of June, Sandor became increasingly excited at the thought of leaving Boise and moving to L.A. with Jeanna. And then, two weeks before graduation, he was told to report to the office of his counselor, Mr. Mackie. Sandor knew there were a number of final details to be worked out about the prom, but when he got to the counselor's room, the door was open but Mr. Mackie wasn't there, so Sandor let himself in. He walked around the office looking at the showcases filled with the trophies the school's athletic teams had won over the years. Then he looked at the handful of college acceptance letters that were framed and hanging on the walls. Not many of the high school's graduates went on to college, so when he realized that Sandor had the potential and the desire to go to college, Mr. Mackie had guided him through every step of the application process. And when Sandor was accepted to the evening division of UCLA, Mr. Mackie was nearly as excited as Sandor and took him out for dinner to celebrate.

Sandor was looking at a copy of his own acceptance letter from UCLA when he heard the unmistakable sound of Mr. Mackie walking down the hallway towards his office. As a young man, Mackie had worked in one of the big copper stripping mines outside of Boise and one day a big piece of machinery had collapsed and crushed his left leg. Despite a half dozen operations, he still dragged his leg behind him when he walked. When Sandor saw the expression on his face as he sat down at his desk, he knew there was a bigger problem than the prom on Mackie's mind.

"What's doing, Mr. Mackie? You look pretty serious there."

"You're right about that, Sandor. I got a letter from the Idaho Department of Education today. It was about your cumulative record and the credits you have towards graduation."

"And we figured all that out and you told me I've got everything I need to graduate."

"Well, yes I did, but I was counting on them to give you school credit for the three months you missed while you were in juvenile center."

"Wait a minute! What're you telling me here?"

"Even though I notated in your record that you completed all the assignments we gave you while you were there, the review board that approves all graduations has decided that you can't get credit for a course when you missed three months of school."

"You *know* that's a load of crap. What about that kid who was in that car accident last year? He missed even more school than me."

"I know what you're saying, Sandor. But not being able to attend school because some drunk runs a red light and smashes into your car is *one thing*. Missing three months of school because you broke a guy's leg with a steel pipe is another."

"Well, did you tell them? Tell them what he was saying about my family! Calling my mother a drunk, saying no wonder my father left us both."

"Yes, I told them. But how many times have we had this conversation before? You've got to learn to walk away from guys who are trying to get on you. No matter *what they say*, you're not entitled to assault them."

"But that was nearly two years ago! I've hardly gotten into any real trouble since then!"

"I know, and that's why I thought they'd let you graduate. But they've taken a hard line with you. It's that new director. He got appointed because of his "get tough" attitude toward so-called school trouble- makers."

"So, that's me? I get lumped in with everybody else?"

"Look, I'm as upset about this as you are. I've already put in an appeal for you. But, to be honest with you, from the way they sounded, I don't know if that's going to accomplish anything."

"And so what the hell does all this mean? Like I've got to go to summer school to graduate?"

"I wish it was that easy."

"That easy! What're you talking about?"

"Summer school is for kids who failed a class because of their grades. They get a second chance to pass their tests. *You* didn't get credit for your classes because you missed too much time, three months. You can't make that up by going to summer school. You're going to have to take all those classes over next term."

"Wait one fucking minute! What're you talking about? You must be crazy! I've got plans! I'm going to be starting UCLA in September. I'm going out there with Jeanna. You know that!"

'Sandor, this isn't up to me. If it was my decision to make, there'd be no problem. But it's not. There's nothing I can really do about this."

"Then just what the hell am I supposed to do? Tell me that, why don't you?"

"I know it's not easy, but you've got to take this as just a temporary setback. Just take those classes in September and you'll graduate in January. Then you can begin the spring semester at UCLA."

"Oh, you've got it all figured out, don't you! Well, that's easy for you to say because you don't have a girlfriend who's going to UCLA *next term.*"

"Jeanna's a wonderful girl. I'm sure she'll understand about all of this."

"Oh, and now you're an expert on women. It must be nice to know everything."

"Sandor, please, I understand that you're very angry right now. But, in life, sometimes you've got to learn to make adjustments. Go with the flow, as we used to say. Look at *me.* When my leg got shattered, I was twenty years old and I thought my life was over but then I decided..."

"Yeah, yeah, I've heard your *leg* story before. I know *all about it!* So just how the hell does that help *me?*"

"Well, with that damned attitude, nothing's going to help you. So why don't you do me a favor and just get the hell out of my office!"

Jeanna was waiting for Sandor outside Mr. Mackie's office and she wondered what they were talking about. She pressed her ear to the door but could hear only their muffled voices. And then a loud crashing sound startled her and she jerked her head away from the door. A few seconds later, Sandor came rushing out of the office and when he saw Jeanna, he brushed past her and walked quickly down the hallway. She called after him but he didn't turn around to answer. He was afraid she'd notice the tears in his eyes.

When Sandor got home from school, his mother was sitting on the couch with a beer in her hand, watching a daytime talk show. She gave him an absent wave of acknowledgement as he dashed into his room and ten minutes later came back into the living room holding his suitcase.

His mother looked up and saw him walking towards the front door. "Just where do you think you're going with that?"

"I've got a problem. I've got to get away from here for awhile."

"What kind of trouble you get yourself in this time...another one of your dumb fights?"

Just then, they heard the sound of a car coming down their gravel driveway. Sandor quickly moved away from the door and walked back to his mother. "Mom, please, you've got to help me. Don't tell anyone I'm here. Tell them I never got back from school. Please!"

"My God, what've you done this time?"

"Please, just do it for me!"

Sandor ran into the kitchen and went down the staircase that led to the basement. His mother heard a knock on her door and when she opened it, a police officer was standing there.

"Afternoon, ma'am, my name's Officer Blodgett. Would your son happen to be home?" "No, officer, he's not. Is there some kind of problem?"

"I'm afraid there is. Would you mind if I come in?"

Sandor's mother led him into the living room. "Why do you want to speak to my son, officer? Maybe it's something I can help you with."

"I'm afraid not. I've come here to bring your son into the station. There's an assault charge out on him."

"Oh my God! Are you sure? What happened?"

"In school today, he assaulted his counselor, Mr. Mackie."

"That can't be right! There's got to be some kind of mistake! Sandor loves Mr. Mackie."

"Well, like I hear it, Mr. Mackie gave your son some kind of news that made him real angry."

"You can't believe how horrible this is! What do you think will happen? Are they going to send him back to the juvenile correction facility again?"

"Records show your boy turned eighteen a few months ago, so considering the trouble he's been in before, this time it could be the county prison."

Sandor's mother's legs started to collapse under her and she sat down on the couch while the officer walked down the hallway and looked in both bedrooms.

"Sorry, ma'am. Just had to make sure your boy wasn't back there, after all. Well, when you do see him, tell him to turn himself in. He'd be making things easier for himself if he did. If we don't see him down at the station by tomorrow morning, we're going to have to go look for him. He doesn't want that to happen."

Sandor's mother silently stared at the old rug on the floor until the officer walked back to the front door. "Sorry I had to bring you such bad news. I'll just let myself out."

Sandor waited until he could see the police car drive away from the basement window, then came back upstairs with his suitcase. When he walked back into the living room, his mother jumped off the couch and tried to slap him in the face. But Sandor grabbed her arm before she was able to hit him.

"How could you have done that to Mr. Mackie after all he's done to help you?"

"*Wonderful Mr. Mackie,* well, he double crossed me. Let them cancel my graduation. Screwed up all my plans!"

"Well, now you've let your temper get yourself in *real* trouble this time. The police are looking for you."

"Too bad they're not going to be able to find me. I'm taking off."

"You can't run away from this. You're only going to make things worse. I'm not going to let you."

"Well, what're you going to do? *Call my father?*"

"Maybe I just *will*."

"So, do you know where the ex-con is living nowadays?"

"Sandor, don't talk about your father that way. That was ten years ago and, besides, he did it for you anyway."

"Like hell! You're the one he did it for, to keep your ass out of jail. That was his big mistake!"

"What'd I ever do to make you hate me this way?"

"Just take a look in the mirror. And when you're sober enough to call him, *wherever* the hell he's living now, you can tell him that I took the van also. Yeah, you can tell him it's my graduation present, only I'm not graduating anyway!"

Sandor let the screen door slam behind him as he walked out with his suitcase and got into the van and drove away. Sandor's mother watched the van until it was too far down the road to see from her front door. She sat back down on the couch and took a gulp from the bottle of beer she had been drinking, then blankly stared at the TV screen until she screamed out, "Now he's gone too!" and threw her bottle at the television. The bottle harmlessly bounced off the screen and fell to the floor and lay there as the beer slowly poured out onto the cheap red rug.

That evening Jeanna was waiting on her front porch for Sandor to pick her up. Her mother stood behind the screen door and watched her daughter bathed in the light of the circular fluorescent light on the porch ceiling. Mosquitoes swarmed above her head but Jeanna's focus was fixed outward waiting for the headlights of Sandor's van to cut a path through the darkness that enfolded their house.

Her mother understood that Jeanna, the one great consolation in her life since her husband suddenly passed away from a heart attack last year, would soon be leaving her to go to California. She loved her daughter and was proud of her success, but in some deep, shameful part of herself, she wished Jeanna would stay home to find a local job and continue living with her family, like most of the other girls who would be graduating this year.

"Sweetheart, are you sure you really have to go out tonight? You usually don't go out on school nights. Is it that important?"

"I couldn't say no, Mom. Sandy still seemed so upset when he called me tonight. I don't know what happened in Mr. Mackie's office, but I've never seen Sandy look like that before."

Jeanna's mother opened the screen door and came out onto the porch.

She walked over to Jeanna and took her hand. "Darling, you know I've always appreciated all the things Sandor did for us after your father died. Sometimes, I think that if it wasn't for him attending to the million and one chores that your father used to take care of, this house would've fallen apart. But the thought of you going off to live with him in California has made me very nervous."

Jeanna put her arm around her mother and they stood side by side looking out into the night. "Don't worry, Mom. Things will work out alright."

"Saying so doesn't make it so."

"How many times have you used that expression with me since I've been a little girl?"

"And how many times have I been right?"

"I know, I'm cursed, oops, I mean *blessed,* with a mother who's almost always right about things."

"I wish I could be as confident about this as you, but I can't help remembering how he sent that boy to the hospital before you were dating him. Anybody with that much anger in him makes me frightened."

"Well, if you had a family like Sandy's, you'd be angry too. Besides, he's always been real sweet to me."

"But you can't compare dating to the pressures of living with a person day in and day out. What if things don't go all that smoothly while you're at UCLA and he's working and going to school at night? What if things happen to upset him or if he's disappointed about how things are going for him? Will he take out his frustration and anger on you?"

"Oh, Mom, Sandy would never do anything to hurt me!"

"Saying so, doesn't make it so."

"Please, Mom, haven't you ever heard of keeping a positive attitude? Sandy says he loves me and I think I love him too. Can't that be enough to get us through the tough times? And, besides, I think I'd break his heart if I backed out on our plans now."

"You're a wonderful girl to be so considerate of the boy's feelings. He's very lucky to have you. But remember what you owe to *yourself,* sweetheart. You've got to consider your own future also. Don't cheat yourself because you're trying to do what's right for *him.* It won't work and you'll only end up resenting him for it anyway."

"Oh, Mom, how did you get to be so smart living here in Boise and being married to the same man all those years?"

"That's exactly how I got to be so smart. I kept on working at it, till I got it right."

Jeanna threw her arms around her mother and held her tight, feeling the support of her solid body as she put her head on her mother's shoulder.

And then the lights of Sandor's van erupted out of the darkness and Jeanna separated from her mother and walked off the porch and out into the glare of the headlights.

Sandor started driving as soon as Jeanna closed the door to the van. From the direction he was taking, she knew they were going to the isolated parking area outside of town where they always went when they wanted to be alone.

"Don't worry, Jeanna. I've got it all figured out."

"Got what figured out? Just what did happen in Mr. Mackie's office today? You looked terrible when you walked out of there."

"Don't worry, I've got a plan. I'll tell you about it when we park."

They drove in silence for fifteen minutes until they pulled into their usual spot off the road that concealed the van behind a large grove of bushes. Sandor cut off the engine and turned to Jeanna with an excited look on his face. "See that suitcase in the back? I'm going to Canada tomorrow. I mean *we're* going to Canada. We can head for Vancouver. I hear it's just like California up there. When I take you home, you pack and I'll pick you up tomorrow morning. What do you think? Great, huh?"

"What do you mean, Sandy? We're leaving to go to Los Angeles in a couple of weeks to set up an apartment before school starts. I've got too many things to do. I can't go on a vacation now."

"I know, I know, but all that's changed now. I'm not talking about a vacation; I mean we're going to *stay* in Vancouver. You can get a job teaching yoga in a health center or maybe start an after school drama program for kids. That's a great idea! That'd be perfect."

"What do you mean *all that's changed now*? Why do you want to live in Vancouver? What happened in Mr. Mackie's office today? Just what did he tell you?"

"Alright, don't get so upset. I've had enough problems today. We're just not going to be able to go to California."

"How can that be? Everything was arranged! You even got admitted into UCLA."

"Yeah, well, that was before the Idaho Department of Education and that Mackie screwed me! I knew I shouldn't have trusted that guy. You think you can depend on someone and then it all goes up in smoke. They're not giving me credit for the time I was in that juvenile center. I'm not graduating now."

"Oh no, that's terrible! That ruins everything!"

"Come on. I *told you* to calm down! We're just going to have to stay in Canada until things blow over a little and then we can go to California in a year or so and you can start UCLA *then*."

"Until *what* blows over? Sandy, did you *do* something today? Did something happen when you were in Mackie's office?"

"So I hit him! He deserved it! Whose side are you on anyway, mine or his?"

Sandor heard the harsh tone in his voice and was afraid he was only making things worse for himself. He reached over and tried to put his hand on Jeanna's shoulder, but she pulled away.

"I'm sorry for talking to you that way, but you know how much I love you. I just can't stand the thought of anything keeping us apart."

"You hit him? Did you hurt him? Are you in trouble?"

"Me? No, no... no trouble. I'd tell you if I was in trouble, wouldn't I? After today, this whole place just leaves a bad taste in my mouth. I need to get away. I'll get my diploma in Vancouver and then maybe we go to UCLA like we planned."

"But, Sandy, they admitted me for September. I can't put it off."

"Sure you can. It's easy! You heard what the plan is."

"That's *your* plan, Sandy. It works for you, but I don't think it's what I want to do for myself. I don't want to go to Canada and teach yoga. I'm all emotionally prepared to leave here and begin the next stage of my life at UCLA."

"Oh, don't give me that psychological bullshit! You just don't want to go with me! You're just looking for an excuse to back out on the plans we made to go to California *together.*" Sandor started to squirm as he felt his shirt began to stick to his sweat soaked back.

"No, you don't understand. I'll go out there first and find an apartment and you can come out when you're ready to leave Canada."

Sandor put his hand to his temple to touch the nerve that had started to twitch over his left eye.

"Or maybe, until you come to Los Angeles, I could just rent a room in one of those inexpensive motels that lots of young people stay at when they move to L.A."

"Oh, sure, like that would really work! You'll meet one of those *pretty-boy* actor types and be shacking up with him in a week!"

"Well, if that's all the trust you have in me, then maybe we shouldn't be living together anyway!"

"I knew it! I knew it! You lying bitch! You never really planned to go out there with me, did you?"

"I've had enough of this, Sandy. Take me home!"

"Take you home! So you can run out on me too? You're no different than all the others! Why did I ever think I could trust you?"

"If you don't take me home right now, I'm going to get out of the van and walk back to town myself."

Jeanna reached for the handle of the door but Sandor grabbed her by the shoulder and pulled her back to him.

"Stop it, Sandy, you're hurting me! Are you crazy?"

"You're the crazy one if you think I'm going to let you go off and screw all those other guys!"

And he put his hands around her throat and started to squeeze. At first she was too startled to struggle but then she began to thrash her arms and managed to scratch Sandor in the face. This only made him angrier and he tightened the grip on her throat until she started to gag. He looked at her eyes as they began to lose focus and drift lazily in their sockets.

Then he took his hands off her throat and buried his face in his hands. Jeanna sat next to him, panting to catch her breath. He looked down at the floor of the van and mumbled, "How could I have done that to you? I'm so sorry! It's just that I can't stand the thought of losing you." And he continued to stare down at the floor as Jeanna jumped out of the van and ran back to the highway to flag down a passing car.

Chapter 13

Sandor headed for the interstate and drove north. He turned on a country rock station and blasted the volume, hoping that in some way it would block out the sound of the thoughts running through his mind. But he kept on hearing that voice. The voice that told him, "You've really screwed yourself this time, haven't you? You can't go back there after what you did today. Two assaults, *in the same day*! Maybe, they'll even charge you with Jeanna's attempted murder! If they catch you, who knows how many years in jail they'll give you? You've lost your chance to graduate and you've lost Jeanna, the only two things that you wanted and now they're gone. What're you going to do now? Forget about UCLA, or any other college. You're just another loser without even a high school diploma to his name. And how're you gonna find another Jeanna? She's the best you'll ever have, and you nearly killed her. And you can't blame this shit on your mom or dad; you did this *all by yourself*."

Sandor opened the window of the van and turned up the radio as loud as it would go, then he drove off into the night heading for Canada. Nobody knew him there, a fresh start in a new country. The second chance he'd always wanted. No talk about his "loser" parents or his violent temper. And when he made a success of himself in Canada, he'd come back home and show everybody how wrong they were about him.

Sandor drove until he needed gas and then bought a couple of Slim Jims and a bag of chips and a coke from the food shop at the station. When he finally needed to sleep he pulled the van off the road and slept in the rear seat. But by the next day the flat sameness of the scenery got on his nerves and he decided if he was driving to Canada he might as well take a route that gave him something to see.

So he waited for the first major road going west and headed for Seattle.

Sandor thought he would drive into the center of Seattle and go up that big tower he had seen on television. But as he drove closer to downtown he soon realized that Seattle was far larger than Boise. He had never been anywhere with so many cars and trucks fighting for driving space. He inched along on some streets, never even getting to the intersection before the light turned red again.

The maddeningly slow pace gave him a chance to look at the people who crowded the streets. He took a close look as they passed in front of his van and rushed in all directions around him. He looked at them and he did not like what he saw. He labeled them as they passed: foreigner, misfit, vagrant, mental case, hustler, hot shot, pretty-boy, little miss hot-to-trot. They couldn't fool him. He knew who they were and he was ready for them.

Tired and angry after trying to negotiate the city traffic for over an hour, he pulled the van into a parking spot a block away from a 7-Eleven. He walked back to the store and picked out a cold ham and cheese hero and heated it for a minute in the microwave. He grabbed a bottle of beer and walked up front to pay.

There were a few people standing on line at the cashier, but Sandor ignored them and walked right up to the cashier. A stocky man in a windbreaker and a backwards baseball cap called out, "Hey, where you goin'? There's a line over here!"

Sandor looked back at him and smiled, then spoke in the calmest of voices, "I am *so* sorry, but I'm in a terrible rush. You understand, don't you?"

The stocky man fell quiet and stared at the ground as Sandor politely thanked him.

And when the young cashier told him that he had to be 21 to buy alcohol he smiled at her also. "Now you're not going to make me walk all the way back to my van to get my proof, are you?" She blushed and handed him his beer.

It was always that easy for Sandor. He was only eighteen, but with his good looks, confidence and his imposing size he was able to get his way. He smiled and spoke in a polite tone of voice, then looked people in the eye with an expression that dared them to say no to him. And the few who did say no were always sorry.

When Sandor finished eating in the van, the thought of spending any more time in Seattle brought a queasy feeling to him. He looked at his roadmap and decided he would drive up the coast until he crossed over into Canada. Then he would head up to Vancouver. Yes, that sounded like a very good plan to him.

Sandor drove until he saw signs that said the border was only five miles away. And then the traffic started to build. The highway in front of him became clogged with cars barely inching along. At first he thought it must be a bad accident, but then he saw a big sign warning drivers that they had to have their identification ready to be checked. Sandor realized that the traffic was caused by the checkpoint at the U.S.-Canada border. He hadn't thought about that. That meant a passport, which he did not have, or checking his driver's license and car registration. What if his mother had put out a report on her van being taken? What if his name came up in their computers as being wanted by the police in Idaho? He couldn't take that chance. He slammed his fist down so hard on the steering wheel that the van swerved into the next lane, narrowly missing a slowly passing car.

Sandor veered into the right hand lane and when he saw the sign that said "Last Exit in the United States," he pulled off the road and then doubled back onto the highway heading south down through Washington. He didn't know where he was headed now, and he was furious at this change in plans. And when Sandor got this angry somebody usually paid the price.

Chapter 14

Sandor drove over 200 miles without stopping before he had to pull into a station to fuel up the van. Looking at the map taped to the station wall, he realized that he was only about an hour's drive north of Oregon. He saw the names that dotted the coast... Astoria, Seaside, Newport, Lincoln, among numerous others, and he felt that somewhere in one of those towns close to the Pacific Ocean was what he was looking for. His mood brightened. He felt a new plan formulating within him. He started to feel in control again.

Sandor paid for the gas and was walking back towards the van when he saw a tall kid about his age standing by the passenger side of the van. He was carrying a big duffel bag and he smiled broadly as Sandor got closer.

"Hey, I don't mean to be any trouble, but when you pulled in here I noticed that you were heading south."

Sandor always appraised a situation before he spoke, trying to determine what attitude might be most beneficial to him. But he sensed no potential threat or danger from this smiling stranger, so he decided to respond in a neutral tone.

"So I *am*, going to drive down into Oregon. Why you asking?" though Sandor knew what he would be asked next.

"Well, I'm headed that way myself. I've been hitching all the way down from Alberta and I sure would appreciate a ride as far as you're going. My name's Jeff." And he smiled again and offered his hand to be shaken.

Normally, Sandor would've smiled back and politely told him to beat it. But despite the stranger's impressive height, Sandor thought there seemed to be something guileless about this Jeff. He'd been traveling alone for so long; it wouldn't be bad to have someone to talk with to break up the boredom. "Guess you got lucky today, Jeff, caught me in a good mood. Maybe I *could* use some company for a while. The name's Sandy. Throw your bag in the back."

They both got into the van and Sandor gunned the engine and headed off towards the coast. Jeff relaxed in the passenger seat and gave no thought to just how long his good luck might last.

They rode in silence for a few miles and then Jeff started to ask Sandor questions about where he came from and where he was headed. Sandor offered as little actual information about himself as possible and then turned the questions back on Jeff, who seemed to have no trouble at all in talking about himself.

Sandor asked what it was like to live in Alberta, and though Jeff told him far more than he wanted to know, he had a way of telling a story that made him easy to listen to. Then the subject turned to sports and eventually music. A little later they discovered they both enjoyed fishing, and that conversation carried them right across the border of Washington into Oregon. Sandor was actually enjoying Jeff's company. It made the time go by faster and since Sandor was driving, he still felt in control of the situation.

They traveled past Astoria in northern Oregon and about a half hour later, Jeff asked Sandor if he was hungry. "Yeah, suppose I *could* use something to eat. Look out for one of those roadside places." Ten minutes later, Jeff pointed out a beat up looking café and Sandor swerved the van off the road into the gravel parking lot. The café was built from weathered boards that had been stained from years of exposure to the heavy winds and constant rain that hit the Oregon coast. It was almost nine at night and since the tourist season hadn't started yet, there were only four other people eating.

Like almost all the other restaurants on this road that paralleled the Pacific Coast, the café had a nautical theme. A large ship's steering wheel was mounted on the wall and each table had a little lamp in the shape of an anchor.

The waitress motioned that they could sit anywhere they wanted, so Jeff headed towards a table near the window. Then she sauntered over and flipped two menus onto the glass- covered table. "I'll be with you two young gentlemen in a minute. Take your time." Sandor looked through the menu. "Looks like if you don't like fried food, you're out of luck."

Jeff held up the menu and pointed to the name, "Hey, this place is called the Anchor Inn. That's because after you eat here you feel like there's an anchor *in* your stomach." Jeff laughed at his own joke and Sandor laughed along with him.

Sandor realized that he was starting to relax. The band of tension that he always felt across his neck and shoulders was less noticeable. Sandor didn't feel comfortable around many people, but there was something different about Jeff. They were roughly the same age and had the same large build, but there was something that went far deeper than that, only Sandor couldn't tell what it was. He admired Jeff's casual manner, his way with a story and a joke. Sandor thought he even liked the fact that Jeff didn't seem to feel intimidated by him. He wondered to himself if that's the way it was between friends.

Sandor took a good, hard look at Jeff as he thought about all of this and then noticed something for the first time. As Jeff held the menu, Sandor saw that Jeff was missing two fingers on his left hand. Not being accustomed to considering the feelings of others before he spoke, Sandor blurted out, "Gee, man, I just noticed your hand. Must've been a bitch of an accident."

"You can damn well say that! Ended up changing my whole life. Maybe for the better, too."

"Whoa, you lost me there. How's losing a couple of fingers turn out to be a good thing?"

"Well, I don't want to bore you with the whole long story."

"No, go ahead. If you don't mind talking about it, I'd like to hear."

"Okay, so it started when my mom got sick and died when I was about six years old. My dad, who was never the easiest guy to be around in the first place, takes this real hard. Now he's got this little kid, *that's me*, to take care of and he's not really interested in that."

"Yeah, I know what you mean, Jeff. My dad ran out on us when *I* was a little kid. "

"My dad probably would've taken off also, but he had nobody to give me to. He started to drink real hard and since he was stuck with me, he couldn't go out to bars or anything at night. So he just stayed home and drank. Sometimes he had his buddies from work come over and they played cards and drank like one million beers. A couple of times it got so rowdy that the neighbors called the cops. It got to be a real mess. Sometimes he'd get up too late in the morning to get me to school. Happened so much the principal called social services and they came over and gave my dad a warning."

"Ahh, Jeff, I feel for you, man. Your mom dies and your father's a real shit."

"And then one day he wakes up late, as usual, and he's afraid to have me miss school *again* so he's rushing like crazy to get me there. He nearly drags me out to the car because he's running so fast. Then he shoves me into the back seat of the car, only he accidentally slams the door on my hand by mistake."

"Oh, damn it! You're kidding!"

"So that was it. They took me away from him and sent me to live in this big orphanage run by these real tight-ass nuns. He came to visit me every now and then the first couple of years, but then he just sort of faded away. I haven't seen him in nearly ten years."

"So you grew up in an orphanage?"

"Yeah, they took care of us pretty good, but they weren't too strong on hugs and kisses, if you know what I mean. But I've got to give them credit; they made sure you got a good education. It was all about praying and studying and if you didn't do a good job at either one, God was going to send you to hell. That's if the nuns didn't beat you to death first."

"Wow, compared to you, it almost makes me feel like I had it easy when I was growing up."

"Well, what can you do? You can't pick your own parents…but you *can* pick what kind of burger you want to eat. Come on, let's order. It's on me."

Chapter 15

By the time Sandor and Jeff finished eating and walked out of the cafe it was pouring. They jumped into the van and Sandor pulled out of the lot and drove south. The rain pounded the windshield and the wipers were barely able to swipe away the downpour before the windshield again became covered in large drops. Sandor hunched forward in his seat and tried to get a better look at the dark, winding road that stretched out in front of them. "So, Sandy, where're we headed?"

And until Jeff asked him, Sandor hadn't given any thought at all to that. If he were still by himself he would have stopped the van when he got tired and slept in the back. "You know, I'm really not too sure. I was just driving."

"Well, it's nearly eleven and the way it looks, it could pour all night. How about us getting some sleep?"

"You're right. I'm beat. Let me find a place to pull over."

Sandor drove another quarter of a mile before he found a turnoff, slowed down, and edged the car to a clear spot on the side of the road next to a billboard. "So, what've you got in mind, Sandy?"

"Well, I was thinking we could sleep in the van. I've been sleeping in the back and it's really not too bad. *You* take it tonight. I'll scrunch up here in the front seat. I'll be O.K."

"Thanks for the offer, but I can't let you do that. Besides, if we stay in the van all night the sound of the rain pounding on the roof is going to drive me crazy."

"Alright, but I really wasn't planning to stay in a motel. I'm trying to nurse my money, but if you…"

"No, no. No motels. We don't need one."

"Then *what?*"

"We're on the Oregon Coast. This is prime vacation property. If this was

45

July or August or a weekend night the place would be crawling with people, but it's a Monday night in June and there are going to be loads of empty cabins all around here."

"But it would cost nearly as much to rent a cabin as a motel room."

"Who's talking about renting?"

Sandor slowly drove the van down the side road until Jeff told him to stop. "Look, over there …on the other side of the stream."

Sandor saw a big cabin behind a cluster of trees. The cabin looked empty. There were no lights on and he didn't see any cars on the property. A narrow wooden bridge connected the road to the land by the cabin. "Looks good, but I don't think it's safe to drive the van across that old bridge. I'm going to pull off the side of the road over onto the grass. Then we can just walk across the bridge."

Sandor slowly edged the van halfway onto the grass before he realized the incessant rain had turned the area into one large pool of thick mud. He threw the van into reverse but the front wheels had already sunk deep into the mud and the van wouldn't move in either direction. Sandor slammed his fist on the steering wheel, "Fuck it! I can't believe this. The damn thing won't move. We're stuck."

"Ah, come on, Sandy. Don't sweat it! It's not blocking the road. We'll shove it out in the morning. Let's just get our gear out of the van and go over to the cabin."

Sandor grabbed his overnight bag from the back and found the big flashlight that he kept in a toolbox near the spare tire. Jeff was already standing on the bridge, waving to Sandor and carrying his duffel bag with his good hand. It was still raining hard but as they walked across the wooden bridge they could hear the stream rushing by underneath them. Sandor turned on the flashlight and pointed the beam of light on the stream. He was surprised at what he saw. "Look at that! Can you believe how fast that water is moving?"

"It's Oregon, Sandy. It rains all the time here because of the mountain ranges near the coast. The clouds move in off the Pacific Ocean, hit those mountains and you've got rain. Then the water runs down off the mountains and runs back into the ocean. It's a real weather cycle."

"You know a lot about that type of shit."

"I got the nuns to thank for banging that kind of stuff into my head. But come on, let's get to the cabin. I'm getting soaked out here."

"Yeah, it's that damn weather cycle."

"Pretty funny there, Sandy. Come on, I'll race you to the cabin."

Sandor got to the cabin door about five steps before Jeff, who arrived slightly out of breath. "Ah, if I wasn't carrying this duffel I would've beat your ass up here."

"Well, maybe next time I'll carry *you and the duffel bag* if it's too much work for you." Sandor slapped him on the back and took the duffel out of his hand and set it on the floor in front of the cabin door. Then he wiped his hands dry on his pants and gripped the doorknob. "Let's see what we got here." He turned the knob but the door didn't open. He put his shoulder to the door and gave a little shove but nothing happened. "It doesn't feel too sturdy. If I really leaned into it I could probably bust it open. What do you think?"

"Nah, let's not do any *real* damage. Here, let me try this. It's worked before." Jeff squatted down, reached into his duffel bag and pulled out a Swiss Army knife. "Can you believe that the nuns gave this to me as a going-away present? It's got a six- inch blade and a million attachments. They said it would be a handy thing to have on my travels."

"I bet they didn't think you'd be using it to break into cabins."

"No sir, but just watch this thing do its magic."

Jeff pulled open a small, thin blade and slipped it into the keyhole in the doorknob. He jiggled the blade a few times and then turned the doorknob slowly. He pushed gently against the door and it opened. "Voila! After you, my dear gentleman." And he held open the door and motioned for Sandor to enter.

In the beam of the flashlight they could see the cabin consisted of one large room with a ladder leading to a loft. Sandor spotted a small lamp in the back of the cabin near the kitchen area. "Let's turn this on. I don't think anyone passing by can see it from the other side of that bridge."

"Yeah, that's good. We could use a little light in here. Hmm, now this place isn't too shabby, is it, Sandy?"

"No, and the price is right also." And they both laughed.

Chapter 16

"Well, I'm beat! Let's check out the sleeping arrangements." Jeff climbed the ladder up to the loft and took a fast look around. He called down to Sandor, "Looks like we might have a little problem here."

"What do you mean, Jeff?"

"Come on up and see for yourself."

When Sandor climbed up to the loft he saw what Jeff meant. "Hmm, only one bed. Well, I suppose one of us could sleep on the floor or out in the van…or maybe in that wooden rocker downstairs. Yeah, I suppose I could do that tonight," he offered.

"Thanks for the offer, Sandy, but I know if *I* did that I'd feel like shit in the morning and so would you. You know… this looks like a king size bed. There'd be plenty of room for both of us. What the hell! It's only for one night."

"Gee, Jeff, I don't know. I feel a little weird about it…"

"Come on! What're you afraid I'll grab your ass? You're not going strange on me, are you?"

"No, no, O.K.., sure, why not? No problem."

"Atta boy, Sandy. I'll sleep on the left side of the bed, if you don't mind. And remember, *no monkey business.*"

And then Jeff laughed and Sandor tried to laugh along with him.

Sandor watched as Jeff took the Swiss Army knife out of his pants pocket and put it on the night table on his side of the bed. He took off his watch and placed it right next to the knife. Then he reached into the back pocket of his jeans and put his wallet on the table. He arranged them so they lay in a straight line on the night table. Then he took off his shirt and jeans and carefully hung them up in the small closet in the loft.

Jeff caught Sandor looking at him. "Okay! So I'm a neat freak. Those nuns ran that place like the Marines. You'd better have everything *just-so* or they'd have your ass. It gets to be a habit. Hey that's a joke! Nuns…habit…get it?"

And Jeff laughed again and this time Sandor laughed along with him.

Jeff went downstairs to wash up and brush his teeth before he went to sleep. When he got back up to the loft he told Sandor, "Bathroom's free, your turn. And before you come back up, do me a favor and turn off the light downstairs, I like it dark when I sleep. Okay?"

When Sandor was finished downstairs he climbed back up to the loft and saw that Jeff was already under the covers. It was hard to make out his face in the dim light that came through the small window in the loft. Sandor took off his pants and tee shirt and crawled under the covers and lay down as close as possible to his edge of the bed. He heard Jeff's voice in the darkness, "Well, this was quite a day. Thanks for the ride and everything else. Get a good night's sleep. Who knows what kind of adventures we'll have *tomorrow*."

Within a few minutes, Jeff's deep breathing told Sandor that he had fallen asleep. He envied Jeff's being able to drift off that quickly. Sandor usually lay in bed for hours as he fell victim to his own dark fantasies and fears. The endless strategizing in his mind to deal with all those people whose motives he couldn't trust. The systematic planning of what he would do tomorrow to make sure he came out on top.

But tonight something was different. He was actually looking forward to tomorrow. Driving with Jeff, having laughs, stopping to explore any place that looked like fun. Who knows where they'd go and where they'd wind up at the end of the day. And maybe, even, no more looking over his shoulder to make sure trouble wasn't creeping up on him. And if any trouble *did* happen to come his way, then Jeff and he would handle it together. Yeah, that's what it must be like when you have someone you can depend on. And with that thought, Sandor closed his eyes and fell asleep.

The next morning Sandor woke up to the sound of Jeff rummaging through the kitchen cabinets downstairs. "Hey, rise and shine up there! Not that there's any sun out yet."

Sandor raised himself up on his elbows and looked out the window in the loft. "Damn! Looks like we're in the middle of a gigantic cotton ball."

"It's the morning fog. It's a killer on the Oregon coast. But don't worry, the sun will burn it off in a couple of hours. I'm trying to find the makings for coffee down here."

Sandor lay back down on the bed and thought about him and Jeff. They could stop at some of the nicer towns on the Oregon coast. Maybe do some swimming if it warmed up. Then head down into California. There must be a million things to do there…could even try surfing. Damn sure nobody back in Boise's going to be surfing any time soon! And when we run out of cash we could get work in a gas station or a fast food joint until we've got enough saved up to move on. Yeah, maybe even work our way down to Mexico…and rent one of those deep sea fishing boats. Catch ourselves a big fuckin' marlin. Then Sandor smiled and drifted back to sleep.

Sandor was awoken by the sound of Jeff searching through his duffel bag. "Sorry, Sandy, didn't mean to wake you. It's still foggy as hell out there, but I wanted to show you something." Jeff handed Sandor a manila envelope.

"What's in it, Jeff?"

"Go on, take a look for yourself. You're the first person outside of the orphanage I've shown it to."

Sandor opened the little metal clasp on the back of the envelope and took out a formal looking letter. He slowly read it and as he began to realize what the letter meant his hand started to tremble slightly.

"That's great, isn't it, Sandy? My college acceptance letter! See, that's my incoming freshman pin attached to it. And it's all paid for by the nuns. They actually set up a scholarship fund for the brightest kids in the orphanage. You can take the money and apply to any college you want, except one of those fancy, expensive ones. They used to tell us they could afford to send one person a year to an Ivy League school or fours persons to a smaller college. Sister Mary Catherine, she's the one in charge of the scholarship program, she'd say that if Jesus had a loaf of bread, would he give it all to one person or divide it into smaller pieces so more could have sustenance. So a small college it is for me, but at least I don't have to spend any more winters freezing in Alberta."

As Jeff rambled on in his excitement, Sandor kept staring at the letter. Then Jeff reached over and pulled another letter out of the envelope. "And look at this. They've already got me in their computers. Jeffrey Maxwell Carter…forget about that Maxwell business. Date of birth, May 10, 1993. Major in psychology! Yeah, I've always been a good judge of people. Interests? …Sex, drugs and rock and roll. Nah, just kidding. It really says people and the environment… thought that would look good on the application. Distinguishing physical characteristics? Exceedingly big dick. Nah, just kidding again…two fingers missing on left hand.

And here's the *important one*. Tuition? Paid-in-full. So, what do you think?"

"What about the time we were going to spend together? The trip down to Mexico?"

"Did we talk about going to Mexico together? I don't think I've got time to do that. I was planning to get to college early. Decide if I want to live in a dorm or find a room off campus. Got to get a part-time job also, unless I want to live on rice and beans for the next four years."

"But we get along so great and I was thinking that…"

"Yeah, we do have some good laughs and I've got about a week before I want to get to college. There's lots of fun stuff we could do on the coast until then."

"Only a week?"

"Well, yeah… but you know what? You can come down to visit me at college. Yeah, maybe on the Christmas break."

"Christmas? That's nearly six months from now."

"Sure, but I've got to concentrate on my grades before then. Not too much socializing. But you'd love it there. Beautiful campus and great-looking chicks, I hear. So what do you think?"

Sandor felt his temple starting to throb, but he managed to look at Jeff and smile and say, "Great, sounds just great."

"Good! Then why don't you come downstairs and get a cup of that spectacular coffee I made? I'm going to take a shower before we leave. There's no rush. That fog is still murder out there."

"No thanks. I think I'll catch a little more rest up here before we go. It may be a long day on the road."

Jeff pulled a towel and some fresh clothes out of his duffel bag and went downstairs to the bathroom. Sandor sat on the edge of the bed and thought about what had just happened. He tried to calm himself. He thought, "It was my fault for being stupid. I let him fool me into thinking he was different than the others. He smiled and laughed and made jokes. Talked about the adventures we were going to have. Tricking me into thinking I could depend on him. And all the time him knowing he was going to leave and go off to college. Yeah, college! Him with that scholarship and *the beautiful campus* and the *great -looking girls*. Yeah, Sandy, why don't you drop around on Christmas and in the meantime have fun sleeping in the back of your van."

Sandor closed his eyes and thought of his own lost dreams; Jeanna and the life they would've shared while they both went to UCLA. And now, Jeff telling him about his fucking scholarship. Rubbing his good luck in his face. Why did other people get all the breaks? If he wanted something he always had to take it himself. And Sandor gripped the metal edge of his bed and squeezed until the pain in his hands made him forget about the throbbing in his head.

Jeff let the hot water in the shower pour over him as he thought about what had just happened. "This Sandy does seem sort of strange and he can get pretty intense, but, hey, he doesn't measure up to *some of the weirdoes* who gave me a hitch since I started out in Alberta. He's really not that bad a guy, and we have some laughs too. I guess he's just a little sensitive. Likes to feel appreciated, well, I can relate to that. I'll pay for his gas and some of his meals; let him make most of the decisions about what we do and where we go. It'll be *fine.* It sure beats looking for a better hitch. And if I play things right, maybe I can even get him to drop me off right at college."

Jeff felt better about things. He rinsed the soap off his face, turned off the water and stretched his hand out from behind the shower curtain to reach for his towel but he didn't feel it on the rack. When he pulled open the curtain, Sandor was standing there holding his towel.

Jeff jumped in surprise. "Yo, fella! You scared the hell out of me there! Guess you don't believe in knocking, but the shower's all yours now. I'm done."

Jeff never realized just how true his words were.

Chapter 17

It was nearly one in the morning and the rain was still beating down on the highway. Tommy peered out the window and saw that the bus was traveling along a road that seemed to be perched on the top of a cliff. It was too dark to see clearly but only a low guardrail separated the road from the drop below.

Reiko slept with her head on Tommy's shoulder; as he looked around the bus it seemed he was the only passenger still awake. The bus was silent except for an occasional whooshing sound as a large vehicle passed it in the opposing lane headed north. Judging from the amount of time they had been driving, Tommy estimated the bus would drop him off at the Stanford station in less than an hour. He would have to gently wake up Reiko and make plans to contact her in San Jose as soon as possible.

Tommy looked out the front window of the bus and watched the frantic arc of the wipers on the rain-besieged windshield. The headlights only seemed to light up the road for a few dozen feet against the rain and fog. Tommy stared at the back of the bus driver's head and wondered how he was able to keep the bus moving so rapidly under such terrible conditions. And then he noticed the rear view mirror that was positioned on the window in front of the driver. As Tommy saw the driver's eyes reflected back at him, he opened up his mouth to scream, but no sound came out. He was staring into his father's eyes.

Tommy grabbed Reiko's hand and started to stand, and as he did, a tractor trailer crossed over the white line and rammed their bus. The impact sent the bus screeching towards the right side of the road. The passengers were all jolted awake and thrown into an immediate panic as they felt the bus swerve on the wet road. Reiko grabbed Tommy's arm and he could just barely hear her voice above the screams of the other passengers.

"Tommy, Tommy, what happened? Are we going to be alright?"

And before he could answer her the bus slammed into the guardrail and plunged off the highway and down the side of the cliff.

The bus careened down the side of the cliff until it hit a massive boulder. Tommy's body shattered the window as he was hurled head first from the bus. He managed to grab onto a twisted dwarf pine tree as he lay sprawled on the ground with his legs dangling over the edge of the cliff. The force of his weight began to pull the roots out of the ground and he slid slowly backwards towards the precipice; then he heard an explosion and looked up in horror as the bus caught fire. He screamed out Reiko's name and tried to get up, but he realized that something had happened to his legs. And then the bus exploded. Just before he passed out he saw a hand with a rocking horse tattooed on it reaching out to pull him off the side of the cliff. He didn't have to look up. He knew who was saving him.

When the emergency vehicles arrived at the scene of the accident they found no survivors in the burning wreckage of the bus. The highway was shut down in both directions and an emergency camp was set up for the long and horrific job of removing the bodies. Trucks lined up on the highway to bring the bodies to the morgue and a helicopter hovered overhead in hopes of their finding someone still alive who needed to be rushed to a hospital. Eventually they signaled to the helicopter that there was no need for it to remain, and it flew back to its home base.

As one medic was standing at the side of the road trying to collect his composure after seeing so many burned bodies, he heard moaning coming from the top of a trail near the guardrail. He rushed over and found Tommy unconscious, lying on the ground. The position of his legs indicated that they were broken. The medic screamed for a stretcher and the helicopter was radioed and told to return to the scene.

As Tommy was being lifted onto the stretcher he opened his eyes and tried to talk. The medic bent down and put his ear closer to Tommy and was finally able to make out what he was saying. It was, "Reiko! Reiko!" and then he closed his eyes again as they carried him away.

As he watched Tommy being lifted onto the helicopter, the medic shook his head and thought to himself, "I hope whoever that poor kid was calling for wasn't on the bus with him because he's the only one who got out alive."

Eddy Donnelly was trying to clear his head as he drove his pickup truck north on 101. He'd been out drinking with his buddies and had just crawled into bed after one in the morning when his phone rang. There had been a huge accident with a bus on the highway and all the volunteer firemen were being called to the scene to help with the bodies. This was going to be something new for Eddy. He had helped with some fires since he'd signed on as a volunteer a few months ago, but nothing where anyone was actually injured. The thought of what he might see when he got to the accident and what he might be asked to do made him wonder if he could really handle the situation.

Eddy didn't know exactly where on 101 the accident had happened, so he drove cautiously, waiting to see the flashing red lights on the emergency vehicles. The rain had let up but the fog was still swirling in front of his headlights. Eddy stared closely at the winding road in front of him and as he slowed down to take a sharp curve he saw something in the distance moving along the side of the road. He was surprised that the pickup's lights didn't scare off the deer but it kept moving towards him. As Eddy drove closer he realized that it was a person, not a deer that was walking along the road. He slammed on his brakes and jumped out of his pickup. He waved at the person coming towards him but the person didn't respond. As the figure got close enough so it could be seen in the headlights, Eddy saw that it was a young woman, an Asian, maybe Japanese, who was walking towards him. And when she reached Eddy she didn't seem to notice him, she just kept walking.

Eddy had never seen anyone in shock before, but the dazed look on her face and large bruise on her forehead told him that she must've been involved in the bus accident. He walked over to her. "Excuse me, young lady, I'm a volunteer helping out with the accident up ahead." And when she stared at him but didn't respond, he gently took her hand and walked her over to his truck. "Why don't you come with me? There are ambulances waiting."

Eddy opened the door and she climbed in. As he pulled away to drive to the scene of the accident, he couldn't help but notice that, despite her condition, the girl sitting next to him was extremely beautiful. Then he sensed something about her, something that made a chill run through his body, and he knew there was only one place he must bring this young woman. And he increased the speed of his truck as he headed for the hospital in San Jose.

In Japan, Reiko's father woke in the middle of the night gasping for air. He sat up in bed and panted as he wiped the sweat from his face. He knew at once that something had happened to Reiko. She needed him and he must go to her. The next morning, with his wife's blessing, he called Reiko's uncle in Vancouver, then told his son to drive him to the airport in Kyoto.

Chapter 18

Tommy's mother slowly began to drift off into sleep. She'd been in room 918 of the South Bay Hospital for the past forty-two hours. In front of her, Tommy lay in his hospital bed. His head was wrapped in bandages and both legs were in casts. As her head slid down and her chin began to rest on her chest, she jerked her hear upward and snapped backed into consciousness. A doctor was entering some information on the chart attached to the bed.

"He's stable. That's the good news. Now we just have to be patient while his body gets itself better."

Lucinda tried to hold back her tears. "Do you have any idea how long that could take?"

"The broken legs, that we can estimate. The coma…well, that's a lot harder to judge. He went through a lot. His head smashed right through that bus window. But you tell me he was a big, strong athletic type. Maybe that will work in his favor, being in condition. It's hard to say, but his vital signs are strong, so we can only hope for the best."

"What can I do, doctor? I just can't sit here and watch him like this."

"Pull your chair over to the bed. Hold his hand. Talk to him. Even if there are no outward signs, he might be able to sense you are here. Sometimes that helps. I wish I could tell you something more reassuring, but I've seen many patients in his condition recover and do just fine. The hard part is the waiting."

So Lucinda pulled her chair over to Tommy's side. She held his hand and, although it was limp, it had the same warm feeling that she remembered. It was late June and she wouldn't have to return to her teaching position in Seattle until September. By then, surely Tommy would be better. That's what she kept on telling herself.

In room 910, Reiko lay in her hospital bed, her face slick with perspiration. She tossed and pulled on the sheets as the dream flashed before her closed eyes. A man dressed in ceremonials robes, so old his face was crisscrossed with deep lines, stood before her bed. His eyes were raised upwards as he chanted a prayer in a strange tongue. Then he turned his gaze downwards towards Reiko and spoke to her in a hushed voice. "Soon your long journey will end. You will be where you belong, with me, at the Village." He held out a dark green and brown flower to her, the strangest Reiko had ever seen. Long full pitchers curved upwards and ended in a rounded head that had two fang-like projections coming from its mouth.

Something about the appearance of the plant brought a sense of dread to Reiko. Then the ancient man threw the flower on her bed and she recoiled from the pungent smell. She was about to call out for help, but then realized she did not remember the name of the person who could help her. The man drew closer to her and whispered, "You will be mine, forever!" Reiko moaned in her sleep and then he was gone.

Finally, after what seemed like a very long time, Reiko felt someone holding her hand. She was afraid to open her eyes, fearing in her half-dreamlike state that she might find the ancient man at the side of her bed. But then she realized there was something comforting and familiar about the touch of the person holding her hand. She slowly opened her eyes and saw her uncle smiling down at her. And in his other hand he held the strange flower she had seen in her dream.

"It is wonderful to look into your eyes once again, my niece. I never would have dreamed that the next time I saw you it would be in a hospital." Seeing the confused look in Reiko's face as she stared at the flower he held, Reiko's uncle told her, "Ah, I found this beautiful flower lying on your bed. Some visitor must have a very special knowledge of rare flowers. They have given you a carnivorous plant, the cobra lily."

And as Reiko sank into an even greater sense of confusion trying to understand how the flower in her dream could now be held by her uncle, she heard a voice coming from the corner of her room and she turned to see… her father. She could not believe that he was here, in California. Still wearing the same type of work clothes he would be wearing on the farm in Japan, he kneeled on the floor facing the window and silently prayed. She knew he was giving thanks that she was not seriously injured in the accident.

Her uncle stood next to her bed, clearly embarrassed by her father's rituals. Dressed in the expensive clothing of a successful businessman, he held her hand and explained how they had found her so quickly.

"Your father called me and said he knew something terrible had befallen you. When I asked him how he could know that, he said I was a fool to question what the spirits had told him while he slept. He said he was flying to Vancouver in the morning to help me find you. He is such a stubborn mule. But this time he was correct in his fears. The airline called to tell me no one had picked up your luggage when the plane landed in San Jose. I called the police there and they told me about the accident with the bus and the Japanese girl who was found wandering on the road. Your father said to me, 'That is my Reiko!' and so we flew here at once."

By now, Reiko's father had finished his prayers and was standing next to her bed. Reiko looked at her father in his peasant's wear and her uncle in his custom made suit and thought how very different they were. But beneath their outward appearances and their different lifestyles and beliefs, they were both the same in the way they loved and protected her.

"My dear father and uncle, I am a very fortunate girl. I am not worthy of your love. Forgive me for the trouble I have caused."

Reiko's father bowed his head. "No, you must forgive *me*, if I have made you feel you could ever bring trouble to me. With every gift of breath the gods give to me, I pray for your happiness."

Then Reiko's uncle's expression became more harsh. "Reiko, you are truly blessed to have such a forgiving father. But, though I too give thanks your injuries are no worse than they are, you must tell me *now*! Why did you get off your plane in San Francisco and why were you on that bus?"

"My father and uncle, I have thought about that since yesterday when I awoke in this hospital and I can tell you with no deceitfulness in my heart that I have no memory of what you say. The last thing I remember, I was on the plane that was to take me to college. The rest is a mystery."

Reiko's doctor entered the room and introduced himself to her father and uncle. Then he motioned for them to walk away from Reiko's bed so he could talk to them privately. "First of all, I want you to know that Reiko should be fine, and unless anything shows up I'll probably be releasing her in a day or two. Her reflexes seem normal and that bruise on her face should be totally gone in a couple of weeks. She went through quite a lot with that horrible accident, so I wasn't surprised that they brought her in here in a state of shock, but she seems much better now."

Reiko's uncle took a step closer to the doctor. "Her memory, doctor, when will it return?"

"Sometimes a loss of memory can be a blessing. She might be better off if she never remembered anything at all about what she saw during that accident. But you can never tell about this type of thing. Maybe she'll start recalling isolated events. Or then again, she could see something that could jar her memory and then it'll all come flooding back to her at once."

"So in other words, doctor, you are telling us that you have no answer for us."

"Maybe not, but I can tell you that from what I've heard about that accident, it was a miracle that she survived."

Reiko's father reached out and touched the doctor just above his heart. "In your world you call it a miracle. To us, we say Reiko is *purotekuteddo*, protected by the gods."

"Then I can only hope your daughter remains *purotekatato*, or whatever, and I hope some of that rubs off on me."

The doctor gave a slight bow and left the room just as Reiko's nurse was entering. After looking at Reiko's chart she introduced herself to Reiko's father and uncle, "My name is Nurse Alvarez, Josanda Alvarez, and I heard the whole terrible story of what happened to your daughter. I want you to know that we will take wonderful care of Reiko. You don't have to worry; she's going to do just fine."

And even though Josanda Alvarez was a young woman herself, appearing not that much older than his daughter, Reiko's father was reassured by her sincerity.

The nurse went over to Reiko and held her hand. "Hello there, my sweetheart, you look so much better today. The doctor says you should try to get on your feet. But because you were in shock, your mind may have recovered, but your body might not have. So you should take a walk to try and get your circulation running and your body back to normal. Don't worry; I'm going to go with you because your legs may not be stable yet."

Reiko nodded and tried to get out of bed, stumbling slightly. She felt as if she were standing up for the first time in years, not days. The nurse quickly grabbed her arms before she could fall. They walked slowly across the room towards the hallway. Then the nurse turned toward Reiko's father. "Dad, would you like to come with us too? Yes, that would be nice." The nurse noticed Reiko's uncle frown and stare at the floor. "O.K. can't leave anyone behind for the first big walk. Let's make it the whole family." And so they all slowly walked out into the hallway.

The nurse held Reiko by the arm, but she had little trouble walking. "You're doing fine, my dear. Your doctor's going to be delighted. Let's go a little bit further and then we can go back to your room." Reiko's father and uncle trailed behind them, nodding their heads happily to see how well Reiko was doing.

Reiko took a few more steps and then stopped in front of the next doorway to a room. They thought she had stopped to rest but then realized she was looking at the patient in the room. His head was wrapped in bandages and both legs were in casts. A woman was seated at the side of his bed holding his hand.

The nurse saw the puzzled look on Reiko's face as she stared at the young man in the bed. "Reiko, this was another passenger on that bus. Do you recognize him?"

Tommy's mother looked up to see Reiko and the two very differently dressed men standing in the doorway. She saw the intense way Reiko was looking at her son. "Do you know my Tommy?"

Reiko looked sadly at Tommy's mother. "I am so sorry that your son is so injured, but no, I have never seen him before."

Chapter 19

The rear seat of Marisa Vargas's old Dodge Dart was covered with mops, brooms, buckets and assorted cleaning products. There was just enough room on the back seat for her 8 year old son, Julio. It was so bright Marisa had to flip down the sun visor so she could follow the winding road leading to the first cabin she had to clean today.

In Mexico, Marisa had been a secretary for her uncle, a successful real estate developer. But, when he was discovered bribing local politicians to speed up the installation of sewers and power lines on his properties, he was sent to jail. Marisa was given the option of testifying against him or risk going to jail herself. So, with the help of a friend who knew how such things were done, late one night she and her son slipped across the border to New Mexico.

Marisa felt that the farther she moved away from Mexico the safer she would be. Her English was poor, so she found herself competing for menial jobs with countless other Mexicans. But by working long, hard hours she always managed to save enough money to enable her to move farther and farther away from the southwest. Until, now, when she felt fairly safe on the Oregon coast, living in Tierra del Mar, a small town near the ocean whose name reminded her of happier years in Mexico.

As she pulled her car into the area she always used for parking, she saw a van parked halfway on the grass. She didn't recognize the van and thought maybe the owners of the cabin had called in repairmen to do some work on the house. She turned to ask Julio to carry her cleaning supplies up to the cabin, but she saw that he was asleep. "God help me," she thought. "suspended from school for fighting again. If only his father had left Mexico with us, then maybe my boy wouldn't be such a problem. Now he's sleeping like he was the king of the universe without a worry."

"Julio, Julio, get up and help your mother. Carry my cleaning things up to the cabin!"

Julio reluctantly roused himself and picked up the mops, brooms and a bucket. He got out of the car and started to walk towards the bridge that led to the cabin, then stopped to take a closer look at the van parked on the grass. "Mamma, look how stupid! Stuck in the mud right up to the top of the hubcaps. They gonna need a tow truck."

"You're right. They must've been here two days ago when it rained so hard. Who knows why workers come on such a terrible day."

Julio raced across the bridge and up the path that led to the cabin. He put the supplies on the front porch and then ran back down to his mother, who was just finishing walking across the bridge. "Mamma, I'm gonna play for a while by the stream. Look for frogs, okay, okay?"

"Yes, fine. Just be careful. And don't go climbing on the rocks too close to the water." Julio shook his head in agreement and ran down along the edge of the stream while Marisa headed up to the cabin.

Marisa had been cleaning the cabin every Thursday for the past six months. The owners came up nearly every Friday afternoon and Marisa had to clean up the mess they made the previous weekend. She reached into her purse and found the key the owners had given her but when she tried to put it in the keyhole, she realized the door was unlocked. Marisa thought, "Those workers truly are stupid. They don't even bother to lock the door." Then she gathered up the cleaning supplies Julio had left on the porch and went into the cabin.

Meanwhile, Julio had found a shallow pool of water right next to the bridge. It was cooler in the shadow cast by the railing of the bridge and he squatted down, hoping to find a frog or, at least, a few tadpoles. But after a few minutes of searching unsuccessfully, he got bored and decided to go back to the cabin to see if there were any good "leftovers" in the refrigerator. Julio had walked halfway back up the path when he suddenly heard a horrible scream. He looked down at the road, thinking an animal had been hit by a car. Then he heard the scream again and realized it was his mother's voice.

Sheriff Joshua Dillon sat on the couch next to Marisa. Her eyes were red but she had stopped crying. Julio stood outside on the porch with Deputy Barney Smithers, who was trying to distract the boy by showing him his handcuffs.

Sheriff Dillon put his hand on Marisa's shoulder and tried to comfort her. "You did the right thing by calling the owners. When they called, they told me you'd be waiting for me to show up. I know it wasn't easy for you to stay here, especially with your son and all, but I really do appreciate it."

Marisa twisted a handkerchief in her hands and stared at the floor. "I never saw nothing like this before. Not here and not in Mexico either."

Sheriff Dillon got up from the couch and walked over to the kitchen doorway. "So this is just the way you found it? You didn't try to clean it up or anything when you saw it?"

"Mi Dios, no! I never touch anything like that. Never!"

"Alright then, I didn't think you did. I know seeing this has been real hard on you, so why don't you and your son just go right on home now."

Sheriff Dillon walked Marisa out to the porch and told Deputy Smithers to take her and her son back down to their car. "And, Miss Vargas, if you can think of anything you or your son might've seen that might be a help to us, just give us a call."

The sheriff watched his deputy walk Marisa and Julio across the bridge and he waved at their car as it pulled away. He waited on the porch until his deputy got back to the cabin. "Gee, Sheriff, what do ya make out of this?"

"Well, Barney, I don't know exactly what happened up here, but it sure doesn't look good. Come on in and take a look for yourself."

"You did say it was pretty bad in there, didn't you? You know I never *did* feel comfortable lookin' at that kind of thing."

"Barney, you know, when your uncle, the mayor, got you this job as my deputy, maybe he should've considered the fact that you really can't handle any kind of blood or violence."

"I told him that, Sheriff, but he said I'd grow into the job."

"Well, you can tell him I think you've reached your full potential as my deputy. Maybe now he can move you on up to something more in keeping with your abilities. I hear the town judge's going to be retiring soon. Maybe your uncle can assign you to that job."

"You know, Sheriff, I asked him just that. But he told me that I'd have to at least go back and finish high school if I was going to be a judge."

"Yeah, I can see not graduating high school being a little bit of a problem right there. So, I guess you're going to be deputying for me for a bit longer. Then why don't you take a look around the grounds and down by the stream? See if you find anything at all that'll do us some good. I'm going to take a closer look inside the cabin."

Sheriff Dillon's father had started taking him hunting and fishing when he was in the first grade so he wasn't the type to get queasy, but he had never seen this much blood in one place before. A trail of blood led from the front porch across the living room floor and into the bathroom. Two towels lay stiffly in a pool of dried blood on the bathroom floor.

In the kitchen a trail of blood started halfway to the kitchen sink and continued up the side of the cabinet doors below the sink. The sink itself was covered in blood and the kitchen wall behind the sink was splattered with bloody streaks. The door to the freezer in the refrigerator was open. The frozen food had melted; leaving a trail of water that dripped down onto the floor and merged with the spots of blood to form pinkish patterns near the empty ice cube trays that lay on the floor.

Sheriff Dillon tried to imagine what had happened. With this much blood there had to be a body somewhere. Maybe it started here in the kitchen and continued in the bathroom, but, then again, there was no trail of blood going from the kitchen to there. The trail seemed to go from the bathroom to the front door of the cabin. And those bloody towels on the bathroom floor. Probably whatever happened, happened there. Then why the blood all over the kitchen sink? Maybe whoever did it was also wounded and came back to the kitchen to clean himself off.

Then the sheriff noticed that the sink had a built-in garbage disposal, the kind that grinds up the garbage as it goes down the drain. He was trying to decide if he really wanted to pry the top off the drain to see what he might find in there, when Barney came running into the kitchen. "Sheriff, you gotta come with me, now! You gotta see what I found!"

Barney led Sheriff Dillon to the bridge and pointed downstream. "Look there, Sheriff, on the branches of that big old tree that're hanging down into the water! You see that?"

Sheriff Dillon saw what his deputy was pointing towards. Caught in the tangled branches, a body bobbed in the current of the stream.

Chapter 20

Doctor Morrissey walked around the dead body on the slab at the morgue and observed it from different angles. "You're right there, Sheriff, no need for an autopsy on this one. He's got five knife puncture wounds in his abdomen, that'd kill just about anyone."

"Yeah, nothing too complicated about it. Guess we can save the taxpayers the expense of calling in the CSI squad. So, Doc, how long ago do you figure this happened?"

"Well, judging by the condition of his wounds and the extent of the body's deterioration from being in that cold water, I'd say about four days ago."

"Right on, Doc. Looks like we're preaching from the same bible. I'm figuring that van stuck in the mud belonged to either this poor stiff or the guy who killed him. We had that hard rain that soaked up the ground just four days ago. So the timing works out just right."

"Got any theories about what happened out there?"

"Well, it's pretty clear that this guy was killed in that cabin and then whoever did it dumped his body off that bridge, thinking the rapids would carry it out to the ocean. He must've done it in the morning when it was still so fogged in that he couldn't see that the body got caught on those branches."

"So if we can identify the deceased here, Sheriff, then maybe you can find out who might've been traveling with him in that van. Well, I'm going to take the usual samples. You can run them through the system and see if you get any matches."

Sheriff Dillon sat at his desk and looked at his deputy's report on the van. "You did a nice job here, Barney. Some nice color photos of the van. This one here shows that the plates had been taken off, and the one of the inside showing no signs of blood or any kind of struggle. They're both just fine."

"Why, thank you, Sheriff, just doin' my job."

"But we *do* need to identify that van so we can find out who owned it. So do you happen to remember anything I might've told you about looking for the serial number of a car when the plates are missing?"

"Hold on there, Sheriff, you're right. Absolutely right! Now I remember. *Look on the engine block.* They almost never know enough to file it off the engine block when they're tryin' to ditch the car. Yes, sir, I'll be right back with that number."

As Sheriff Dillon leaned back in his chair to wait for Barney to return with the serial number of the van, he realized that the waiting had just begun. Unless the computer checks identified the dead man or the owner of the van, there wasn't much else he could do.

Five days later, Matt Connors was sitting in his office in La Jolla, California, writing out the monthly statements for his clients. He'd bought a Lawn Doctor franchise two years ago and had established himself as one of the few non-Mexican or Japanese landscapers. A fact like that made a difference to some of the old families in the area who still believed that "America is for the Americans."

Connors hated computing the monthly bills for his services. It seemed the wealthier a client was, the harder it was to get him to agree to the number of hours his lawn had been worked on. Connors knew that the bigger the bill, the longer the time his customer would put off paying it. He always seemed to be doing this compromise between asking for the amount of money he had rightly earned and a lesser amount he knew would be paid on time and without much complaint.

He was trying to decide just how much money he could extract from a particularly argumentative client when the phone rang. He put it on speakerphone so he could continue to work on his bills. "Lawn Doctor, Matt Connors here."

"Matt, hello, it's Donna. Please don't hang up!"

When Connors heard the voice of his ex-wife he slammed his accounts receivable ledger shut and grabbed the receiver. "Look, what is there about *never call me again* that you don't understand?"

"Matt, I'm sorry. I know I promised, but you've gotta listen, this is different!"

"Yeah, I'm sure it is. It's *always* something different. You're very creative when it comes to thinking of new reasons for asking me for money. Well, Sandor is 18 years old now, so *that's it*! You're not due any more child support for him."

"Matt, you don' understand. I'm *calling* about Sandor. I just got a call from a sheriff in Oregon. He told me that they've got Sandor's body. Sandor's dead, Matt. Sandor's dead."

"Damn it, damn it, what're you talking about! How can he be dead? How can he be in Oregon?"

"I didn't want to call you, Matt. I didn't want to bother you. But Sandor signed over the van to himself last week and he just took off and left. He's been missing over a week."

"And you didn't tell me?"

"I didn't know what to do. You told me not to call you anymore."

"Christ, and now you tell me they found his body in Oregon. God, I can't believe it!"

"They told me I gotta come up there to identify the body. Tierra del Mar, on the coast. I can't do it by myself, Matt. I just can't see him that way by myself. You gotta meet me there."

"I can't do that, Donna. I just can't leave everything and go up to Oregon."

"You gotta do it, Matt. No matter what went on between me and you, he's still your son, too. You gotta meet me there. I need you."

The next morning, before dawn, Matt Connors was in his pickup driving north through California. He was driving over a thousand miles to meet Donna in the Portland airport. He wondered just how big a mistake he had made in agreeing to drive to Tierra del Mar with her. Nearly a three-hour drive together, with the sour history they had between them, going to see the body of their dead son. Days don't get any harder than that.

The last time Matt Connors had seen Donna and Sandor was four years ago. He'd been working for a landscaper in Phoenix and decided to surprise them both by driving to Boise for Sandor's fourteenth birthday. He knew his marriage to Donna was long a thing of the past, but he still had hopes of salvaging some kind of a relationship with his son.

They had lived together until Sandor was only four, then Matt had to leave to "go away on work." The few times Sandor did agree to talk to him on the phone he was angry and hostile. Two years later, when Matt came home, he knew he wouldn't be able to live with Donna anymore and no matter how hard Matt tried to make things good with his son, Sandor never forgave him for being away.

And the outcome of the surprise fourteenth birthday appearance shouldn't have been a surprise at all. Sandor threw his father's still-wrapped birthday present on the kitchen table and went out to spend the night with his friends. Another thousand-mile trip, and for a ten- minute visit. That was all that Matt could take. He never saw Sandor again.

Donna's plane from Boise had landed an hour before Matt got to the airport in Portland. He found her near the baggage pick-up area, sitting with her face in her hands. He walked up to her and quietly called her name, and she looked up at him with a grief-written expression. But even though her eyes were brimming with tears, Matt hadn't seen them this clear in years. No sign of the usual hazy look caused by whatever mixture of alcohol and drugs she could get her hands on. Gone straight...now that it was too late to make a difference for Sandor.

Donna stood up and put her hand on Matt's arm. "Oh, Matt, I can't thank you enough for coming. This has been so, so hard for me. I can't believe things have come to this."

Matt hadn't felt the touch of Donna's hand in so many years that it surprised him that this alone was enough to fill him with regret. She wasn't forty yet and despite the years of destructive and neglectful behavior, he could still see remnants of the beautiful young woman he had met in high school. Now that she could meet his gaze because she no longer had a substance abuse problem to hide, it made his sense of loss all the more palpable. And now, here they were, brought together again by the death of their son. "I know. Even though things were no good between Sandor and me for a long time, this is still tearing me up inside. I know it's got to be even worse for you."

"Oh, Matt, I feel so guilty. I was so bad to him. Just so bad..."

"It's all right, Donna. You did the best you could. Don't be too hard on yourself." He placed his hand on her shoulder and then she put her head against his shoulder and cried.

Ten minutes later, they were sitting in a lounge in the airport. Matt asked the waitress for a beer but Donna only wanted a tomato juice.

"When Sandor took the van and left, I knew I had to straighten my self out. I haven't had a drink in over a week. It's not much, but it's a start."

"You know, Donna...I still blame myself for what happened to us. You were pretty together till you started to hang out with me. I never had too much trouble controlling my drugs; a little pot at night, maybe party with some coke on the weekends. It was just fun, a nice way to unwind. But you got *way* into it. If I had known that would happen, I never would've let you get involved in the first place."

"I know, I screwed up, *big time.* I'll never forget what you did for me... You know you didn't have to do it. I asked you not to."

"I didn't do it just for you. I did it for Sandor also. I always figured it would be harder for a little kid to be without his mom than his dad. Besides, like I said, I felt responsible for getting you involved in that drug scene...so I took the rap for you... both of you. Two years in the state pen for dealing weed....." Matt took a drink of his beer, then started to drum his fingers lightly on the table. "But what really killed me was the way things were when I got out."

"I didn't lie to you, Matt… Billy was yours. Why couldn't you believe me?"

"Why? Cause the timing didn't add up to me. Here I'm locked up and all of a sudden you're pregnant and you're telling me it happened just before I was sent away. Maybe and maybe not, the way I figured it. And besides, the way you got when you were stoned, I don't think you'd even remember who did it to you."

Donna reached for Matt's beer but he pulled it away from her. She stared down at the table and shook her head. "Damn it, Matt, you never even seemed to give a god-damn when Billy was killed! Didn't it mean anything to you?"

"How could it? I never even really knew the kid. And besides, you were giving me that crap about Sandor killing him on purpose. Things aren't bad enough between us and you're calling my nine-year-old son a murderer."

"You didn't know him the way I did. He was so moody. And it seemed like he was always angry. As far as I was concerned, he was capable of it."

"Well, maybe he had something to be angry about, with a father who wasn't there and a mother who couldn't stay sober two days in a row."

Donna recoiled as though Matt had just slapped her in the face. She turned away from him and took the paper napkin on the table and started to slowly tear it into long even strips. She looked inconsolable. Matt had another drink of his beer and looked at his ex-wife. If he had intended to devastate her, he had done a thorough job. If she had come to the airport tonight crushed by the news of Sandor's death, he had only accomplished making her feel that much worse. He had some major grudges against Donna that maybe he still needed to settle, but he decided this wasn't the time to do it. He couldn't stand to see Donna in any more pain than she was in now.

Matt reached across the table and took her hand. "Look, I'm sorry. I shouldn't have said those things to you. It's just that I'm feeling really miserable myself. There's no point in us blaming each other…it's too late for that."

Donna looked at Matt and gave him a sad smile. "Thanks, Matt. I couldn't stand to have us be mad at each other now."

Matt paid for the drinks and they both walked slowly into the airport corridor. It was now after midnight and the airport seemed deserted.

"Well, Matt. What now?"

"It's way too late to drive to the coast. We'd better stay at one of the hotels around the airport tonight. We can get an early start in the morning."

Matt carried Donna's overnight bag for her as they walked to his car in the garage. Then they pulled into an EconoLodge they saw as they exited the airport. There were only a handful of cars in the hotel's lot so they knew they'd have no trouble getting a room. The young, sleepy- eyed clerk at the reservation desk turned down the sound of the jazz station he was listening to on his portable radio and asked Matt and Donna the same question they'd both been individually asking themselves. "What type of room you folks lookin' for?"

Matt and Donna looked at each other. Then Donna turned to the clerk and said, "Make it one with a double bed." She turned towards Matt again. "Is that okay with you?" He nodded, "Yeah, that'll be fine."

The clerk offered to show them to their room but Matt handed him a $5 bill and told him they could find it themselves. When they got to the room, Donna asked if she could use the bathroom first. She and Matt tentatively kissed and then she took her overnight bag in with her and shut the door. Ten minutes later when she came out, she found Matt fully dressed and asleep on the blanket of the bed. Donna didn't try to wake him as she quietly got into bed. She knew it was probably better this way.

Chapter 21

The sun shining through the worn curtains of the window in their hotel room woke Matt and Donna at six the next morning. While Donna showered, Matt made them both coffee from the little brewer in the room. A half hour later they were on the road and headed for Tierra del Mar.

They didn't speak much during the trip. Donna rested her head on the door window and tried to fall back to sleep. Matt turned on the car radio, low enough not to wake up Donna, but just loud enough, he hoped, to help him keep his mind off what he would be seeing at the end of the car ride.

It was nearly 9:30 when they pulled up in front of the police station. When Matt and Donna walked into the station, Sheriff Dillon was sitting at his desk, expecting them. He stood up and offered his hand to both of them and motioned for them to sit in front of him.

"You must be Mr. and Mrs. Connors. I'm so sorry I had to ask you to come up here for such a terrible thing. But we've really got no choice. We need to have your boy officially identified."

Matt cleared his throat and managed to say, "Thanks, Sheriff. I understand how this works. But tell me, because I still don't know. What happened to him?"

"Before we get into all that, why don't you come with me and have a look at your boy. Let's get that done first. Now, Mrs. Connors, you needn't come also, if you think it'll be too hard for you."

Matt looked at his ex-wife's stricken face. "That's right, Donna. I'll do it. Is that what you'd like?"

She reached out and took Matt's hand. "Thank you both, but I came all this way. It's important for me."

Sheriff Dillon asked them to follow him and they walked down the long corridor that led to the coroner's office. Inside, the coroner was standing next to a table holding a body fully draped with a white sheet.

Donna grabbed Matt's arm with both of her hands. The coroner stood there impassively, making Matt wonder if he had ever had any children of his own. "Alright, folks, just tell me when you've seen him long enough." As the coroner reached over to pull the sheet away from the body, Donna dug her nails into Matt's arm. And when the face of the body on the table was revealed, she gasped. "Oh my God, that's not Sandor!"

Matt took a step closer to the body. "What the hell, that's not my son!"

Donna reached out towards Matt and embraced him. "Thank God! He's alright, he's alright." They held each other tightly, both overwhelmed by their relief. Then Matt gently separated from Donna and turned towards the sheriff. "How did this happen? Why did you think this was our son's body?"

"First off, let me tell you I'm happy for you folks that that's not your boy. But we still may have a problem here."

"Problem, what kind of problem? And you still haven't told us why you put both of us through this agony by telling us our son was dead."

"You're right. We've got a lot to talk about. We'd better go back to my office. This might take a while."

Seated back in Sheriff Dillon's office, Matt angrily gripped the arm of his chair. "You've got a lot to answer for here, Sheriff."

"You know, Mr. Connors, you seem awfully angry because that's not your son out there. Would you have felt any better if it was?"

"Of course not! What kind of a stupid question is that?"

Sheriff Dillon looked at Donna. "Your husband's awfully upset, and I can understand that. But he's going to have to calm himself down if any of us are going to get our questions answered here."

"He's right, Matt. Let the sheriff tell us what happened."

"Thank you, Mrs. Connors. Now I'd like you to take a look at these photos." He handed Donna two snapshots and Matt leaned over to look at them also.

"Well, there are no plates on this van, so I can't be sure, but it looks like my van."

"You can be sure that it *is* yours. We checked the serial number off the engine. We found it about five miles from here, empty, stuck in the mud. Registration check came back with your son's name on it."

Matt put the photos back on the sheriff's desk. "And just what in the hell does my son's van being stuck in the mud have to do with that dead body anyway?"

Donna leaned over and patted Matt's hand, attempting to calm him. "Yes, Sheriff why *did* you think that was our son?"

"Just taking a calculated guess."

Matt jumped out of his seat and took a step towards the sheriff's desk. "You just *guessed it was my son!* What kind of man are you!"

"You've got quite a temper there, Mr. Connors. I would've thought that two years in the penitentiary in Idaho would've taught you to control it just a bit."

"Wait one damn minute! How the hell do you know anything about me?"

"I wouldn't be much of a sheriff if I invited someone into my office without finding out what kind of person was coming in here. Just being prudent."

"Well, that was over ten years ago and I don't need to listen to any of that from you!" Matt got out of his seat and headed for the door of the office.

"You can leave if you want to Mr. Connors, but then you'll never find out anything about your son. Is that what you want?"

Donna turned towards Matt, "Please stay! Do it for me."

Matt stopped in the doorway and reluctantly walked back to his seat. "Look, Sheriff, I don't know why you've taken this attitude towards us. You made a mistake about our son and instead of apologizing, you're acting like you want to interrogate us."

"Then let me get to the point, Mr. Connors. We found your son's van across the stream from a cabin, a cabin covered in blood. And when we searched the surroundings, we found that body you've just seen, with five knife wounds in his stomach."

"What're you trying to say, Sheriff?"

"The prints on that body didn't come up with any matches in the data bank. We didn't have any idea who it was. But we did know who owned that van, your son. That left us with only two possibilities."

"Just wait one god-damned minute! You've got no right…"

"Let me finish, Mr. Connors. Two possibilities…either the dead body was you're your son, or…your son was the one who killed that boy."

Matt half rose out of his chair. "Look, you can't go jumping to conclusions!"

"Maybe so, but if it wasn't your son who did this, then why were the plates taken off the van to cover up the identity of the owner?"

The question hung in the air for a few seconds before Donna replied. "Sheriff Dillon, our son is missing, isn't he? Haven't you considered the possibility that whoever did this has harmed our son also?"

"Fair enough question and I can't rule that out…yet. But let me ask you both to think about one thing, and I hope you can answer me honestly considering what's at stake here. Is there anything at all in your son's past that might lead someone to believe he was capable of killing that boy?"

And as Donna and Matt stared at each other, their silence filled the room.

Chapter 22

The young man walked up to the information desk at South Bay Hospital. "Excuse me. I'd like the room number of the Japanese girl who was brought here after that bus accident a few days ago. You know, the girl who was in the news."

The elderly volunteer who manned the desk two days a week looked up at the pleasant looking young man. "Yes, I know who you're talking about. That did cause more than the usual excitement around here. Terrible thing, that bus accident. Too bad more people couldn't have been saved. You'll never catch me driving on that road at night and in the rain. No, not me. But you know, we've actually got another."

"Yes, I'm sure you do, but you see, I'm in kind of a hurry. So if you could just tell me what room she's in."

"Well, hospital regulations... you a doctor or a relative?"

"No, no, I'm more important than that. I'm the guy who saved her life."

Reiko was finishing packing her bag when she saw the young man standing in the doorway talking to Nurse Alvarez. He was staring at her with a broad smile. Nurse Alvarez announced to Reiko, "Normally, we wouldn't be allowing a visitor just now, but I know you'll be happy to meet him and express your gratitude to him."

As Reiko wondered why she would want to thank this man she had never seen before, he took a few steps into her room. "Hi there, Reiko, what an improvement! You can't imagine what you looked like the last time I saw you."

Reiko closed her suitcase and took a hard look at the man. "Excuse me, but I do not recognize you. My memory of things still has not returned. Please be kind enough to tell me how I know you."

"You don't remember me! Now, that comes as quite a surprise to me. You'd think that with what I did for you, my face would pop right out at you."

"I am very sorry, but can you please now tell me who you are?"

Well, I'm just the guy that saved your life, that's all. Eddy Donnelly, the guy who found you walking down the highway and brought you to the ambulance."

"Oh, yes, my uncle told me. So, you are the man who did that kind thing for me. I am glad you came, so I can thank you. My father and uncle will be here shortly and I know they too are very grateful to you."

"Thanks, Reiko. I was only doing my job, would've done it for anybody. But, you know, when I saw you out there on that road, a beautiful girl like you, and I helped you the way I did, well, I've been feeling like a certain kind of a *connection's* been made, if you know what I mean. I read about you in the papers, even saw you on the local news, and I'm thinking that, well, there was something so special about the way we met, that it would sort of be a shame to just let it go at that."

"Excuse me again, but I am not so sure what you are saying to me."

"Well, the nurse told me you're going to be leaving the hospital and I was thinking it would be real nice if we could get to know each other a little better."

"Oh, I think I now understand what you are meaning. And, and…though I am sure you are a very nice person, I do not think that would be possible."

"Not possible! And just why would that be?"

"I am leaving this place right now. I must be going to college. I should have been there already. My father and uncle are coming with a car to drive me to college. We are leaving today."

"Oh, it looks like my timing isn't very good. But if you're going to school in this area maybe we just might bump into each other again. It happened once, right? It might just happen again."

"Yes, yes, that would be a pleasant surprise. I do not mean to be rude to someone who has been kind to me; only, my father and uncle will be waiting for me now."

Eddy Donnelly waved goodbye to Reiko but as he began to leave he turned to say, "Maybe some other time!" and then walked off towards the elevators down the hallway.

Reiko picked her bag up off the bed and started to walk towards the door just as Nurse Alvarez was entering the room. "You know, that Eddy fellow who just left seemed like a very decent guy. Maybe you should try to stay in touch with him."

Reiko took a step backwards in surprise at what she felt was the nurse's intrusive suggestion. "Yes, I am grateful to him, but there is just something about him that made me feel uncomfortable."

"Oh, I wouldn't worry about him. I was speaking to him before he went into your room. He seemed really nice to me, really nice. Like someone you could trust, if you know what I mean."

Reiko was beginning to wonder why the matter of Eddy seemed to hold so much importance to the nurse, but then she was disarmed by Alvarez's warm smile as she said, "Your dad and uncle are downstairs with the car. I'll be missing you, Reiko, but it's time for you to go."

Nurse Alvarez took Reiko's suitcase in one hand and held Reiko's hand with the other and they walked towards the elevator. But as they passed by room 918, Reiko motioned for the nurse to stop. Reiko stood in the doorway and saw that nothing appeared to have changed in the three days since she had first been to this room. The boy's mother was seated in the chair next to the bed and the young man wrapped in bandages still appeared to be in a coma. The boy's mother stood and came over to Reiko. "Good luck. I see you're going home. I looked forward to your little visits. It did me good to see someone make such quick progress. It gives me hope that one day my Tommy will walk out of here just like you."

"Yes, I know that one day it will happen for you. You must keep on believing this."

"Bless you, Reiko. I'll be praying for you." And as Tommy's mother gave her a long hug, Reiko blushed bright red.

When Reiko and the nurse finally reached the street, they saw Reiko's uncle behind the wheel of a large sedan and her father in the passenger's seat. Reiko turned to the nurse and started to shake her hand. "Thank you so much. You have been so kind to me."

The nurse put down Reiko's bag and gave her a big hug. "A handshake! You must be kidding. Ooh, you're going to have to get used to us Americans and all our hugging! Now, good luck, Reiko. You'll have all of this behind you in no time. But, if you ever need anything, any kind of help, you can always find me here. Just ask for Nurse Alvarez. You remember that, Nurse Josanda Alvarez."

Reiko's uncle got out of the sedan and came over to get her suitcase and to shake the nurse's hand. "Thank you for taking such good care of my niece. I wish we had nurses like you in Vancouver."

"I know...I'm one in a million. Now be good to your niece or you'll be hearing from me."

Reiko's father got out of the car and bowed to Nurse Alvarez. The nurse waved goodbye to him as he, Reiko and her uncle got back into the sedan. As the sedan began to pull away, she called out, "Now you two gentlemen take care of my girl."

Reiko's uncle had studied the map of the area carefully, so he knew exactly which streets would lead him back to the highway that would take them to San Jose. And as they drove, Reiko, her father and uncle were so involved with discussing their plans for the day that they didn't notice that their car was being followed by a man driving a pickup truck.

Reiko's uncle wasn't comfortable driving at the high speeds of a typical California driver, so when he got on Highway 101 heading south he stayed in the right lane for the entire ride. That made it easy for his car to be followed all the way until he left the road at the San Jose' State University exit. Now Eddy knew exactly where to find Reiko... all he had to wait for were the instructions telling him when to do it.

Chapter 23

When Sheriff Dillon got no response from Matt or Donna to his question about any possible history of violence in their son's past, he decided a different approach might be more effective. "I'm sorry if I seem a little harsh. I do have a boy of my own, so I should've appreciated how hard this has been for both of you. You've heard a lot this morning. Why don't you step outside the station for a while and talk this all over? I know you could use the time to yourselves."

Matt quickly walked out of the station with Donna trailing behind him. As soon as they got to the parking lot he turned to her. "I just can not accept this! That guy has already got Sandor tried and convicted and he doesn't even really have the slightest idea what happened out there!"

"Look, Matt, I know what you're saying, but I wish I could be as convinced as you. *Somebody* killed that poor boy and left our van in the mud."

"I can't believe it! You're as bad as that sheriff!"

"I'm sorry, Matt. I just don't know what to think. But I lived with Sandor all those years; you didn't. And all I know is that sometimes he'd give me a look that just sent a chill up me. And then there was the whole thing about…"

"Oh, no, you're not going to bring that up again?"

"I can't help it. You know what I always thought happened to Billy."

"Well, you just better keep your damned mouth shut about that because he's walking over to us right now!"

"So, Mr. and Mrs. Connors, have you thought of anything that might…?"

"Look, Sheriff, first of all, you can stop calling us Mr. and Mrs. because we're not married any more…"

"Matt, there's no reason to bring that up now."

"Excuse me, but nobody made me the wiser till right now. So, maybe that explains why you two don't seem to see eye to eye on things."

"No, no, don't try that with us. We're in perfect agreement about this. We may not know why he was up here in Oregon, but we know he's in some kind of trouble. Somebody stole our son's van and then murdered that boy you showed us. That's who you should be looking for."

"Well, if that's the case, Mr. Connors, where's your boy and why hasn't he contacted the police about the van being stolen? You know, if what you say happened is so, I'd really hate to think the worst about what happened to your son."

"Sheriff, I have to have faith that my husband, okay, ex-husband, is right about this. I just feel our son's out there somewhere, and he needs help."

"Yes, can I help you?" The admissions officer at the bursar's office looked up from her computer screen and saw that a tall, good-looking young man was next in line to see her. He stepped up to her desk and smiled at her. "Yeah, sure, I hope this is the right place. I've already taken a little tour of the campus before I found your office here. I've got a college admissions packet and they told me this is where I could do early registration."

"Absolutely, you start here first. So, let me start off by welcoming you to San Jose' State University. If you don't mind my taking a look at those papers......Hmm, yes, here you are in our computer. Jeffrey Carter, major in..."

"Psychology."

"That's right, we've got it here. And I can see that your tuition has been paid in full for the year, so no problem there. Now tell me, are you going to be living in one of our dorms, because if you are..."

"No, no thanks. I've already rented a place in town, but maybe you could give me some information about hooking up with a roommate."

"Later this afternoon we're having an orientation meeting for the incoming freshmen over at Jerry Brown Hall. You'll get most of your questions answered over there and you just might meet someone who's looking to share expenses on a room."

"I'll be there. And thanks for your help."

"That's what we're here for, Jeff. And we're finished now. Take this bursar's receipt and you can go into the auditorium on the first floor to register for your classes. Oh, oh, but wait, one more thing. Did you get your freshman pin? One of these."

"Ah, well, that does look familiar, but I don't really think I have it with me."

"Don't worry, take this one. You know, this was my idea. Tried it for the first time last semester and it proved to be very popular. Lets the new students identify each other. Sort of an icebreaker type of thing. Makes it easier to make new friends at school."

"Well, who can't use some new friends? Thanks for thinking up the idea."

As Sandor gathered his papers he smiled to himself at the ease with which he was able to slip into the identity of Jeff Carter, and when he turned to go, he saw the next person waiting in line was already wearing the freshman pin. "Well, *hello*! How'd *you* like to be my new friend?"

And the beautiful Japanese girl blushed bright red.

Reiko's father and uncle stood outside the San Jose' State University Administration Building while Reiko was registering. Her uncle looked out at the large grassy oval in the center of the campus and watched the young men and women walk from building to building. "Now I feel satisfied. Reiko seems to have fully recovered and this looks like it will be a good place for her, at least for now."

Reiko's father nodded but said nothing. He looked around the campus, as though he was searching for something he knew was there, but could not see.

"Yes, I know," said Reiko's uncle, "I would have liked a more prestigious college also. But with good grades, Reiko will soon be able to apply to a school more in keeping with her abilities. Stanford is just miles from here."

"No, you still don't understand. The school is not my worry. You can worry that for yourself. *Reiko* is my worry. What can happen to her? How many times can she remain *protected?*"

"Protected! Oh, I forgot what a foolish man you can be! People here do not believe such things. You must remember that you are not in Japan anymore."

"Who is the fool who believes that the gods care *which side* of the ocean our Reiko is on? Why else do you think Reiko does not lie buried now, like the other passengers on that bus?"

"Please, I am as happy as you that Reiko is safe, but I do not give credit to *invisible spirits in the sky.*"

"Then I will have to pray for both of us that Reiko remains protected!"

"Ah, you are such a stubborn man. But, then, yes, pray for both of us if you think that will help Reiko."

As they stood there discussing Reiko, suddenly she walked out of the Administration Building. She smiled and waved when she saw her father and uncle, then walked in their direction.

Reiko's uncle nudged her father. "Look, I have not seen such a smile from her since we have been in California. See, she is already happy with being here."

But then they noticed the tall young man walking alongside her.

"Father, uncle, everything has gone so well. I have already registered for all my classes with the help of my new friend. It would please me to introduce him to you."

"Name's Jeff, happy to be of help to your daughter. I know how confusing things can be first day on campus." He smiled and held out his hand to Reiko's father and then her uncle. "And if you don't mind, I'd like to show her where the college bookstore is."

"Yes, please, father and uncle, I would like to do this now. Can I meet you by the car later?" And before her father could respond, Reiko and Jeff walked off along the path leading to the next building.

"See how foolish it was to worry. She is already meeting people and making friends."

"All the more cause for concern."

"What do you mean? When did you learn to become so untrusting?"

"Someone who walks through life with his eyes closed would ask such a thing. We have no idea who this is she goes off with."

"Who is this Jeff? He is a student at this college. She will be back in a few minutes. What more do we need to know right now?"

"I need to know who this Jeff is, who he *really* is. If he is someone from whom Reiko must be protected."

A month later, Reiko hoped she had put her father's fears to rest. She and her father had established a routine of meeting at six o'clock in the morning and jogging for three miles along the streets of San Jose before the early morning traffic congested the roads. Reiko was an experienced runner but she still had trouble maintaining her father's pace. His years of discipline at studying martial arts along with the leg strength built from laboring on his farm, made it easy for him to negotiate the hilly terrain they traveled each morning. Reiko labored to keep up and had to take deep breaths to recite the morning prayers with her father as they ran.

Each morning their run ended at the Rise N' Shine Coffee Shop. Reiko and her father sat in the nearly empty shop at "their" table that faced the well-tended garden of flowers just on the other side of the shop's window. Reiko would drink a cup of the strong coffee she had come to enjoy, while her father had a glass of herbal tea imported to his amazement, from Japan. Reiko's father would often take a paper towel and gently pat his daughter's forehead dry. He himself seemed to make so little exertion on his morning run that someone seeing them sitting together might have thought he had been idly drinking his tea and waiting for Reiko to arrive at the shop after her run. And more than one observer might have been surprised to learn that the relationship between the attractive young woman and the older man of somewhat indeterminate age was actually that of father and daughter.

Usually, he would start their conversation by asking her how she was progressing in the courses she was taking, demanding to know what assignments she needed to complete for each subject. She would patiently reassure him that she was doing very well in all of her work and there was no need for his worry. Then, Reiko might ask of her mother's health or how her brother was doing with the managing of the farm and question how much longer her father might feel the need to stay in San Jose.

"Your uncle has been generous enough to give me the funds to stay here until I feel comfortable enough to leave."

"And what might give you the peace of mind to do that, Father?"

Reiko's father reached across the table and took her delicate hand. "This boy, Jeff; tell me things about him that will quiet my doubts."

"He's good to me, Father. He treats me as though I were special."

"So, if nothing else, he is perceptive."

"Father, not every man feels the world should revolve around me, as you do. But Jeff, yes, sometimes he reminds me of you in that way."

"And what does he remind you of, the other times?"

"Ah, you are so persistent with your suspicious mind."

"And what of those *other times?*"

"Then it is all about him and his plans and his dreams. And I like to be with someone who is focused on the future and their own success."

"You find comfort in what is yet to be?"

"Far more comfort than in thinking of the past and all those people on the bus who died while I was saved."

"Does that night enter your thoughts often, my Reiko?"

"Too often, Father."

"Then perhaps you are ready to agree with me that there is something very important for you to learn from that night."

PART 2

PROTECTED

Chapter 24

Five months had passed since Donna had returned to Boise. Five months with no news about Sandor. Was he still alive? And, if he was, where was he and why wasn't he contacting her? She had played over the possible scenarios in her head a hundred times, but the ones with the bleakest outcomes were the ones that most frequently recurred. Then, late one Tuesday in the middle of November, all that changed.

"Hello, Matt, it's Donna. I'm sorry if I woke you, but I've got important news."

"Oh, Donna, no, that's okay. I was still up. Yeah, important news, what do you mean?"

"It's Sandor! I've heard from him!"

"Donna, my God! What did he tell you? Where is he?"

"I don't know where he is, but he sent me an email."

"What'd he say?"

"I'll read it to you. 'Mom, I know I ran out on you, but I needed to get away. Guess what? I'm in college. Bet you never thought I'd make it. Your college boy, Sandor.' "

"I knew it! I knew he was out there somewhere, and look... he says he's even going to college. Seems like he's done alright for himself."

"Matt, have you lost your mind? Sure, if he really sent that email at least it means he's still alive, but it doesn't explain what happened up in Oregon."

"Okay, you're right, Donna, but it's still so great to know he's alive. That seems like the most important thing right now."

"Matt, I know you just can't stand to think the worst of Sandor and even though I give you a tough time about it, I want you to know that I really do appreciate the way you defend him. It helps give me some hope that he'll come out of this alright."

"Well, I'm glad to hear you say that, because I've been thinking about the way I talked to you when we were in Oregon, and I'm not too proud of some of the things I said to you."

"I know, but don't worry about any of that. This has been damned difficult for both of us to deal with."

"You know, Donna, I wish you had taken me up on my offer and come back to LaJolla with me. Maybe some good could've come out of all of this. I think we're both a little older and wiser than we were before."

"I'm more than a little bit older but I'm not so sure about the wiser part. I've been wondering what it would be like if we were together, and I liked the idea of it, but I can't trust myself yet. I needed to come back here to Boise and make sure I could stand on my own two feet. I just couldn't afford to depend on you to take care of me like in the old days. So, anyway, you'll be happy to know that I'm working as a cashier in the town mortgage and loan office."

"Now, that *is* good news, Donna. I'm happy for you."

"Thanks, Matt. Cleaning myself up and now holding down this job, it's been really important to me. And it helps get my mind off Sandor for a while each day."

"I know what that feels like and it's great he wanted you to know that he's out there and doing something that you'd be proud of, but we still don't know where he is. He intentionally didn't want us to be able to contact him."

"When I emailed him back, my letter was returned undeliverable. He made sure he sent it from a computer that couldn't be traced. Well, I'm going to contact Sheriff Dillon and let him try to find out where the email came from."

"Sheriff Dillon! Donna, you can't be thinking of doing that! That man's convinced Sandor killed that boy. We can't do anything to help him find Sandor. Don't you understand that?"

"If you think that's such a terrible idea, then just what *are* we supposed to do?"

"We've got to wait. Wait for him to feel more confident about his surroundings and then, hopefully, contact you again. And maybe that time he'll give you more information about where he is."

"And then?"

"Then I go find him and help him with whatever trouble he's in."

Things had also changed for Marisa Vargas since that day over five months ago. She dreaded what she might find each time she went to clean a cabin. She would unlock the front door and stand in the entrance and peer into the cabin until she felt it might be safe for her to enter. Her nights were filled with nightmares of men jumping out at her from behind the furniture and dragging her screaming into the bathroom.

When her actual screams in the middle of the night woke up Julio and made him run into her room to see what was wrong, Marisa decided that she could no longer clean homes for a living.

In early November, when the tourist season is over and the Oregon coast begins to slip into a nearly six month long period of gray skies and constant drizzle, one of the waitresses at the Anchor Inn decided that she would lose her mind if she had to endure one more bleak northwestern winter and quit to move to Arizona. Due to this, Marisa found herself waiting tables.

When Marisa told the owners of the Anchor Inn that she would no longer be able to clean their house, they fully sympathized with her reasons. And when the waitressing job opened up, and they remembered what an efficient and reliable worker she had been and also that she had a young son to support, they offered her the job immediately. She cautioned the owners that she hadn't been a waitress since her college days, but they told her she'd have plenty of time to "learn the ropes" during the long, slow winter season.

The only problem was they needed her to work at least one day of the weekend. "That's alright, but I don't know what I would do with Julio on the day I work. He's still too young to leave at home by himself."

"Don't worry about that, dear," said Sophie, one of the café owners. "Bring him into work with you. Its quiet this time of year, he won't get in the way. So, he'll do his homework, and maybe he can even help clear the tables. It'll give him a sense of responsibility; now, that can't be a bad thing."

That is why on the Saturday after Thanksgiving, when Sheriff Dillon came into the Anchor Inn to have his lunch, he found Marisa standing behind the counter and Julio sitting at a table in the rear reading a book.

"Well, I'll be! Isn't this a surprise. Just when did you start working at the café? And that's your boy over there, isn't it?" The sheriff sat down at his usual table by the window so he could get a good view of the highway passing in front of the café. Marisa came over and offered him a menu but he waved it away. "I think I must have that thing just about memorized by now, but tell me, how did this all come about?"

Sheriff Dillon shook his head sympathetically as Marisa told him why she wasn't able to clean houses any more. "I can appreciate what you must've been going through. I think you did the right thing for you and your boy by giving it up and coming to work here. Now the worst thing you got to worry about is guys like me complaining the coffee isn't hot enough."

"Thank you, Sheriff; you have a kind way about you."

"Hey, now don't let that get around. People are supposed to be scared of me, you know."

Julio heard this as he was about to put the silverware and a glass of water on the sheriff's table, "Not me. I'm not afraid of you. That's right, I even got my own sheriff's badge."

Marisa put her hand on her son's arm. "Julio, please. Don't talk to Sheriff Dillon that way."

"Oh, that's all right, Marisa. We're only funning one another. So, you've got your own official badge, uh?"

"Sure, I wear it when I come to work at the restaurant, in case somebody gives my mom trouble. See, I wear it right here on my pocket."

"Hmm, that is an interesting pin, sorry, I mean *badge*, you've got there. Got three initials S...J...F. What's those letters stand for?"

"Well, the S is for Sheriff and the J is for me, Julio and the F is for...I don't know, but it looks good, don't it?"

"It sure does. So, your mom buy that badge just for you?"

"Naw, I found it. Found it by that cabin."

"That cabin? Which cabin would that be, Julio?"

"You know...the one with all that blood."

Marisa grabbed Julio by the arm and pulled him towards her. "When did that happen? You never told Momma about that"

"I found it that day the sheriff and his deputy came to the cabin. I never told you because I thought you might take my badge away if I did."

"Well now, son, I think I've got a good idea. I'd like to take that badge of yours back to my office and take a closer look at it. So, how's about you loan it to me and in return I'll give you an authentic Deputy's badge. How's that for a fair trade?"

"A real, honest to god deputy badge! You promise?"

"You know a sheriff isn't allowed to go back on his word. So, the quicker you give me that pin, the quicker I can go back to my office to get you your deputy badge."

When Sheriff Dillon got back to his office he found his deputy sitting with his feet up on the desk. Barney abruptly got up when he became aware of the sheriff staring at him. "Whoops! Sorry 'bout that, Sheriff. Didn't hear you walkin' in here. Boy, you're just like a cat on your feet."

"Barney, how many times I've told you not to sit that way? It looks real bad when a citizen comes in here."

"You're right, Sheriff. You'll never catch me doing that again. You can count on it."

"Seems like I've heard that before. Well, anyway, take off your badge and give it to me."

"Ah now, Sheriff! You can't be firing me just for putting my feet up on the desk. Come on! You gotta be givin' me another chance. My uncle's goin' be real upset about this."

"Hmm, firing you! I never thought about that. I wonder, can I *do* that? But, *no,* Barney, I just promised to loan your badge to Marisa's boy because he found something that might turn out to be important. Take a look at this. He found it at the cabin the same day we found that body in the stream."

"S...J...F, gotta be somebody's initials, but who? We oughta call the owners of that cabin because if that pin belonged to them, then it isn't a clue at all."

"Now you're thinking Barney! But if it isn't theirs, then who did it belong to? Since we still don't know the name of the boy who was killed, it could be his initials."

"Now wait a minute, Sheriff! Those people who came up here to look at the body, didn't you say their son's name was Sandor? Maybe that's what the S on that pin stands for."

"Alright, Barney, you are really on fire today! How could I ever have thought of firing you?"

Matt Connors was waiting for a call from one of his biggest customers, so when the phone rang and it turned out to be Sheriff Dillon he was doubly disappointed.

"Hope I'm not disturbing you, Mr. Connors. It's Sheriff Dillon...from Tierra del Mar."

"Yes, Sheriff, I *certainly* remember you. Do you have something important to tell me because I'm sort of busy right now?"

"To be honest with you, Mr. Connors, I'm not too thrilled to be talking to you either, but I haven't been able to reach your ex-wife on the phone, so I thought I'd give you a try. First off, have you seen or heard from your son since the last time we spoke?"

"Of course not! Don't you think we would've contacted you if we had?"

"Not really, but I just thought I'd ask anyway. But there was another reason I called. Do the initials S...J...F mean anything to you?"

"No, why? Should they?"

"Maybe. We found a pin at the scene of the crime that had those initials and we wondered if that sounded familiar to you, seeing how your son's first name starts with an S."

"So you call me up from Oregon to get some evidence you can use against my son! Well, you can go to hell, Dillon! And if you haven't noticed, my son's name is Sandor Nathaniel Connors and that sure doesn't add up to S...J...F."

"And maybe *you* haven't noticed that we've *still* got an unsolved murder and an unidentified dead body up here in Oregon."

"And since *you're* the sheriff and I'm not, I guess that's *your problem*, not mine. Good night, Sheriff Dillon."

Chapter 25

Reiko looked at her watch and realized that she was going to be late to pick up Jeff. The traffic was heavier than usual today and it had taken her longer than she thought it would to drive to the gas station and fill up the car her uncle had leased for her before he returned to his business in Vancouver. She hoped she would be able to make up some time when she left the busy business section near the station and drove back towards the quieter part of town where Jeff was renting an apartment.

Reiko could have saved a little driving time if she briefly used the highway to get to Jeff's apartment, but she always avoided the major road. Though she still remembered nothing of the night of the bus accident, even driving on any part of the highway caused unanswerable questions to flood her mind. Why was she on the bus that night and why, alone, had she been saved?

Jeff always became upset when she wasn't on time. Reiko had seen him lose his temper and it was something she wanted to avoid causing. Jeff could be intimidating in a way that reminded her of her uncle, who had always demanded excellence from her. She had come to experience this form of behavior as an indication that her best interests were behind their complaints.

Jeff would tell her that she had to have a plan for the day. That she didn't want to leave things up to chance. She needed to take *control* of the situation or she couldn't blame anyone but herself if things didn't work out the way she wanted. "Focus!" that's what he always said to her. "You've got to focus on what your goal is and then eliminate all the things preventing you from achieving that goal."

Reiko felt that Jeff was preparing her for something crucial in her future. She didn't yet understand what that might be, but she was glad for the opportunity to benefit from Jeff's discipline. Of course, there were other reasons she was happy to be with Jeff. She was attracted to his probing intelligence and handsome features and muscular body. She could relax with him, forget about the pressure of getting the superior grades her family expected of her; they knew how to laugh together. She also felt a compelling sense of energy emanating from him. He always seemed completely absorbed with her when they were together. If anything else in the world mattered to him, he didn't show it. Yet he wouldn't yield control of the relationship to her, and so she gave herself fully to this man whom she believed was fully her measure...never before feeling so enthralled.

When Reiko pulled up in front of Jeff's apartment she was twenty minutes late and he was pacing up and down in front of the building. Reiko got out of the car and quickly walked over to him. "I'm late. I know. I'm sorry. I should have left earlier." She leaned over to kiss Jeff, but he pulled away. "Oh, you're angry with me. I made you wait in the street."

"No, no, I know you're late, but that's not it. It's one of those damned headaches again. I slept for two hours this afternoon but it didn't go away."

"Oh, I'm so sorry. What can I do for you?"

"The way I feel, I'm not fit company for anyone tonight. Why don't you go to town without me? I don't want to ruin your night. If I start to feel better later I'll meet you at the NightOwl."

"Are you sure? I can come up and give you a massage. That might make you feel better."

"Thanks, babe, sounds tempting. But I think I really need some time to myself here."

"Okay, Jeff. I'll wait for you at the NightOwl until midnight. I hope you can make it." Reiko got back in her car, pulled out into traffic and drove away.

Sandor stood by the curb and waved at Reiko until her car was out of sight. When he walked into the living room of his apartment, his roommate Antonio was sitting on the couch with his young girlfriend, Lola. They were watching wrestling and Sandor heard the unintelligible taunting of the wrestlers screaming at one another as the crowd roared in the background. Then there was silence as Antonio put the sound on mute. "So, you ditch your beautiful girlfriend again? What's the matta, Jeff, she's not good enough for you? Antonio'll take her off your hands. Whata' you say?"

Lola gave Antonio her best version of an indignant look and gave him a hard shove in the shoulder with all the force she could muster with her two thin arms. "What you mean with that fresh talk! If you don't shut up, *I'm* the one gonna be changing loverboys. How's that idea sound to you, Jeff, baby?"

Antonio threw his arm around Lola and squeezed her close up against his side. "Hey, I got an even better idea. Why don't you get your little Japanese girlfriend up here and maybe we could all get *really friendly together*, if you know what I mean."

"Antonio, you dumb fuck! If I didn't need your share of the rent money I'd kick you out on your ass!"

"Well, when you win the lottery, let me know. I'll start packing."

When Antonio turned on the sound of the wrestling match again, Sandor walked into his room and shut the door. He lay down on his bed in the dark and closed his eyes but he could still feel his head throb. The sounds of the television coming from the living room became intolerable. He jumped off the bed and swung open his door. "If you don't shut that fucking thing off I'm going to break your arm!"

In the months they had lived together, Antonio had learned just how far Sandor could be pushed without it becoming dangerous. He understood it didn't pay to press his luck over something as meaningless as the volume on the TV. He remembered what his dad had always told him, "Pick your fights, don't let your fights pick you." So he turned down the sound of the TV until he could hardly hear it himself.

Sandor went back into his room and walked over to the window. It looked out onto the tree- lined block of two- story houses that were rented mainly by other students at the college. It was dark, but a full moon helped compensate for the dim light cast by the street lamps. Sandor looked out the window, but in the darkness of his room, he could see his reflection staring back at him. He'd been playing the role of Jeff for so long that sometimes he was nearly startled to see his own reflection.

His game had been a success. He'd fooled everyone. He was getting good grades in his classes and he had a knockout of a girlfriend who was crazy about him. But she was crazy about this guy Jeff. Jeff's way of kidding around and being confident without being too pushy. Jeff's way of being casual and being able to take what comes in stride. That was Jeff. It wasn't Sandor, and keeping up that image was becoming harder and harder. Whenever he lost control of himself and let some of his anger get the better of him, he saw Reiko recoil. How much longer could he keep up the pretense before she saw him for who he really was? As much as he hated that jerk Antonio, at least he could be himself with him. Antonio didn't know it, but he was the one who got to see the most of the *real* Sandor.

Sandor knew that the battle he waged within himself was the cause of his headaches. He probably shouldn't have tried to take on Jeff's personality. Who would've known the difference? But Jeff had seemed so happy, so carefree. Sandor couldn't resist hoping he could remake himself in Jeff's image. This would be the new start he had always hoped for. Maybe he could learn to control the violence and anger that always seemed to be seething just below his surface. Besides, what choices did he have? Give it all up and leave school and lose Reiko, just like he lost Jeanna? To go where and do what? No, his best chance was to hope no one discovered what had happened to the real Jeff…at least until he had planned his next step.

Sandor thought of going to meet Reiko at the NightOwl, but he knew with the way he was feeling, that would be a mistake. He lay back down on his bed and closed his eyes. His head pounded but now his hand also began to throb. He could still feel the fingers he had cut off, even though that was over five months ago. He was shocked when he first had that feeling and when it persisted he did some research and found out it's common to people who lose a part of their body. It actually has a name, the phantom limb syndrome.

Sandor knew that if he was going to pass himself off as Jeff, he had no choice. At the time it seemed a small price to pay, and it still did, except for the pain that seemed to come and go, in sync with his headaches. Sandor had remembered the movie he had seen about the mountain climber who was trapped in an avalanche in the Himalayas. His arm had been wedged under a boulder in the ice and freezing cold. The only way the climber could free himself before he froze to death was to cut his arm off. And because the arm was completely numb from being frozen for days, he felt no pain when he did it.

That movie had flashed into Sandor's mind that morning in Oregon, nearly six months ago. After he had thrown Jeff's body into the stream, he went back to the cabin and filled up a bucket with ice from the freezer in the refrigerator. He put his hand into the bucket until he had no feeling in his fingers. Then he took the same knife that he had used on Jeff, and used it on himself. And he even laughed as he did it, thinking of the horrified expressions on the face of the nuns if they realized how their parting gift to Jeff had been used.

Sandor thought back, trying to imagine just how overwhelming his anger was, to have done this. Just how betrayed he felt when he heard that Jeff would be going off to college by himself. Just how big a fool he felt for thinking of all the adventures Jeff and he were going to have together, when it turned out Jeff would have no time at all for him. Sandor didn't feel that sorry about what he did. After all, it had led to his being in college and meeting Reiko, but it did frighten him. Frighten him because he had no faith that he'd be able to prevent himself from killing again. And who would his victim be the next time?

Sandor was surprised how easily he had adjusted to the missing fingers, but the continued pain from his hand and his headaches were making him miserable. He reached into the night table drawer and pulled out the plastic container that held the prescription painkillers he had bought from Antonio. He had come to need the medication so frequently that he was able to gulp down three capsules without a drink of water.

As the painkillers started to take effect, Sandor's thoughts started to drift and soon he fell into a deep sleep. He lay on his bed, sweating and tossing and eventually he started to dream. He was looking out a window watching the landscape rush by. He realized he was on a train and he was able to see himself sitting there. He was a little boy and the compartment was filled with adults who were eating and drinking but ignoring him. And then suddenly he was outside the train, running along the tracks. He looked up and saw his mother and his brother Billy sitting in the train. He yelled their names but they couldn't hear him. Then his brother turned and looked at him and Sandor heard him say, "I'm with Mommy now, and you're not." Sandor ran out of breath and as he slowed down the train started to pull away from him. When the last car passed him the conductor stood at the rear railing and held out his arm to Sandor, but he couldn't grab onto it. He wasn't able to make out the face of the conductor but he could hear him laugh as the train sped off into the distance.

Sandor awoke with a start and bolted upright, only to see Lola sitting at the edge of his bed, staring at him. "Man, you must really have some nasty dreams!"

Sandor shook his head, trying to clear his thoughts. "What're you doing in here, Lola? Antonio's going to be really pissed at you."

"Ah, I'm not worried about that big baby. He's in his room, zonked out on pills, as usual. And please, do me a favor, when I'm not around him, don't call me Lola. He gave me that name cause he thinks it's a hot name for a chick. Call me Margrita. It's who I really am."

Sandor felt a sudden connection to this girl who, like him, was pretending to be something she wasn't, but before he did anything rash that he'd be sorry for later, he stood up and motioned for Margrita to get off his bed. "You know, I never did believe that tough-girl act you put on when you're with Antonio. Something in your eyes told me that was just an act. What're you doing with that guy? "

"Look, Jeff, I don't know what kind of family you came from, but for me, Antonio is a step up. He's going to college, for God's sake! My family's lived in Watts forever! Do you know Watts? I bet you don't! And being Antonio's girl is a lot better than livin' back home and havin' to watch out for my older brother tryin' to put his hands on me. Yeah, you heard that right!"

"You're kidding me about that, right?"

"Damn if I am! But anyway, Antonio is just for now. I know there's better guys out there for me than him."

"For a girl like you? You bet there are."

"Well, you know, I know a better one already. So, maybe what I'm sayin' is if you and your girlfriend ever break up, not that I'm wishing that on you, but, you know, just keep Margrita in mind. Antonio is just for now."

"That's sweet of you, but maybe I'm not really that much different than Antonio anyway."

"No, I seen you with your girl when she's up here with you and I can see you're real good to her. Besides, I can tell you're a decent guy. My friends always say I'm a real good judge of character."

"Thanks, but maybe you're not as good a judge as you think. But, come on, we'd better get out of my room before Antonio wakes up and finds you in here. I really don't have the patience to deal with him tonight. And besides I've got to get down to the NightOwl now."

"What, your girlfriend waiting on you down there?"

"Well, yeah, she is. We made plans and I got to get there."

When Sandor walked Margrita back into the living room he saw Antonio's jacket hanging from the kitchen chair. He picked up the jacket and began to go through the pockets, but then he heard the door to Antonio's room open. Sandor looked up and saw Antonio standing in the doorway holding his car keys in his hand. "You lookin' for these, my friend?"

"Well, yeah. I need to borrow your car tonight. I'd really appreciate it."

"All of a sudden you're nicey, nicey with Antonio when you need a favor. Well, Antonio would like a favor too. Like maybe a hundred bucks off on his rent this month. Then you could go for your car ride tonight. You could even take Lola with you if you want. Maybe you'd like that."

"A hundred bucks! I could rent a car for less than that."

"Now that's a good idea. I hear there's an Avis down by the highway. You could probably walk there in about half an hour."

"Okay! Screw you. A hundred bucks off on the rent this month. Just give me the damn keys!"

"Here they are, big man. And if you bring back Antonio's car with no damage I'll even throw in some of those beautiful pills you gobble down so fast."

Sandor ran out into the street and started up Antonio's car. Reiko had gotten to the NightOwl after 8 o'clock, so she would've been waiting for Sandor for almost two hours by now. Maybe some friends from school were hanging with her, or maybe she was alone, but if she said she was going to wait until midnight, she'd still be there.

When Reiko had arrived at the NightOwl someone was waiting for her. Someone standing in the shadows near the rear of the bar watching the door and hoping Reiko would be coming. He knew there was something special about tonight and his opportunity would never be better. And when he saw her walk in by herself this time, he felt tonight would be his lucky night.

Eddy Donnelly watched Reiko as she stood near the entrance to the bar and searched for familiar faces in the crowd. His heart dropped when she noticed someone waving at her and walked over to a small group of people and sat down at their table. Eddy watched them talking and laughing, then someone ordered a round of beers and then a little later, another round. He was prepared to wait until his chance came and at 10 o'clock it arrived. The other people got up to leave and after exchanging hugs, Reiko sat back down at the table. She nursed her glass of beer and began to watch the nightly local newscast on the TV perched on the wall next to her.

Eddy could see that stories about a liquor store holdup and a possible increase in real estate taxes didn't hold Reiko's attention. But then the newscast switched to a feature with a correspondent at the side of a highway with a group of people standing behind him. Some of the people were holding flowers and others were holding lit candles. The camera panned to a young woman holding a sign that said "DANNY WE'LL NEVER FORGET YOU." An older man was holding a sign that said "Lights Save Lives." Reiko's head snapped to attention as the reporter started to speak. "Tonight is the six-month anniversary of that horrible bus crash that claimed the lives of 38 passengers last summer. The relatives and loved ones of the people who perished on the bus that night have come together here for a roadside vigil. Not only as a way to publicly pay their respects as a group for the first time but also as the beginning of an initiative to get the county to reduce the speed limits on our highways and also install improved lighting on the roads."

Eddy watched Reiko stare at the TV screen and he knew the time was right for him. He walked up behind her and said. "I still can't believe how lucky you were that night." Reiko turned around in her seat and stared at Eddy. "It's me! You must remember me. It's Eddy. I'm the one who found you walking along the road that night."

Reiko finally took in what Eddy was saying. "It *is* you. What're you doing here? Were you looking for me?"

"Me? Looking for you? No, no, just a coincidence. I don't live too far from here. Come here pretty often. Here it is, the sixth anniversary of that accident and I'm watching the TV and I look down and see you sitting there. It must be fate. I *had* to come over and say hello. Say, do you mind if I sit down?"

"No, I suppose not. Please sit down. I have been thinking more and more about that night. Then I see the people on the road with their signs and then I see you. Maybe it *is* fate for me to talk to you. Even though I do not know you at all, you are my closest connection to that night."

"You're darn right I am. I was there when you needed help. I'm the only one who knows what things were really like."

"What can you tell me? Do you know something that can help me understand why so many died, but I was saved?"

"Well, I…I don't know if I can help you with that. But I know what I *can* do. I can take you back there tonight. Right to the spot where I found you on the road, and then I'll drive you to the scene of the accident. Maybe some of those people we saw on the news will still be out there. Maybe they know something that will help."

"Yes, I think you are right. I need to go there. I feel I escaped the fate of the others for a reason, but I am haunted by what that reason might be. If I go then maybe I will understand. Will you take me there now?"

"Sure, Reiko, sure. It's only about a thirty-minute drive from here. My car's right outside."

Just to be cautious, Reiko walked over to the bartender with Eddy. "Jamey, I'm leaving with Eddy here, to go out to where that bus accident happened. You will remember that?"

"Sure thing, Reiko. I've seen this guy plenty of times around here."

Eddy smiled at Reiko, "I can see you're a careful lady, and I don't blame you. But you've got nothing to worry about."

As they walked to Eddy's car, Reiko thought about Jeff. She had been waiting for him for over two hours and she thought about calling him before she left the NightOwl with Eddy. But when he got one of his bad headaches he often slept for twelve hours straight and she didn't want to take the chance of waking him. But just as importantly, she had never told Jeff that she had been in that bus crash. It was a part of herself she needed to keep private. She had tried to accept herself being saved while so many others died as a stroke of great fortune. But she could not stop the words of her father from going through her head. He was convinced there was a reason, far beyond their understanding, why she had been saved. Something inside of her was telling her he might be right.

It was nearly 10:30 when Sandor drove into the NightOwl's parking lot. He was pulling Antonio's van into a spot when he saw Reiko and a man walk across the lot and get into a car and pull away. Sandor couldn't believe what he was seeing. He had always trusted Reiko, or at least as much as he could trust any woman, but seeing *this*, his first impulse was to speed after them, cut in front of the car, and force the driver to pull over to the side of the road. But if he did that, Reiko would probably give him a story about her being tired from waiting for him to show up and this guy was just giving her a ride home. He'd never really know if she was telling the truth, and knowing himself as he did, he knew that would plant a seed of doubt about her in his mind that would grow to poison their relationship. Sandor decided that the smartest thing he could do would be to follow their car at a discreet distance until they arrived at their destination. Then he would know what to do next.

Eddy drove out of town and got on 101 heading north. Reiko watched in silence as the dark road curved and wound its way through deeply wooded settings. After another ten minutes, Eddy slowed down and pointed to the road in front of them. "Over there! I'm pretty sure that's where I spotted you. See, it's across from that rest area. I'm going to pull over."

When Sandor saw them stop, he pulled over and turned off the van's engine and switched off the lights. He could barely make out the figures of Reiko and the driver of the car. Now Sandor knew one thing for sure, Reiko wasn't being driven home. But why did they come out here? There was only one reason he could think of to stop at a spot on this deserted stretch of road. But he'd better be wrong about that, or they'd both be very sorry about what would happen.

Reiko looked out the window of the van and shook her head. "No, this place does not tell me anything. I feel it would do no good to look further here. Would it be possible to take me to where the bus crashed? It is late and maybe they are all gone now, but I feel that is where I need to go."

"Sure, if that's what you want. We can do that. I'm here to help you, just remember that." Eddy pulled the car off the curb of the road and continued north.

When Sandor thought they were out of earshot, he turned the engine of the van back on and followed them at what he felt was a safe distance. He had turned off his lights, but the full moon lit up enough of the night so he was able to keep on their trail. They continued driving north and the further they got from San Jose, the angrier Sandor became. He couldn't think of any excuse Reiko could make that would convince him that there was anything innocent about her riding with another man at 11 o'clock on a Monday night, heading farther and farther out of town.

Sandor followed their car for another ten minutes and then saw them pull off the side of the road and get out of the car. Sandor stopped his van and watched as Reiko and the man walked over to the side of the cliff. He saw a number of small lights flickering on the ground around them, but he couldn't understand their purpose. Then the man pointed down over the side of the cliff and when Reiko moved closer to him he put his arm around her shoulder.

That was all Sandor needed to see. He jumped out of his van and ran towards them.

Reiko and Eddy heard someone running and when they turned around

Sandor was on top of them. Eddy was startled, and before he could say more than "What the fuck..," Sandor punched him in the face and knocked him down. Sandor stood over him and kicked Eddy in the side.

Reiko screamed, "Stop it, Jeff! Stop it!" and grabbed his arm, but he pushed her aside. Eddy tried to crawl away, but Sandor reached down and yanked him back up onto his feet. Eddy hit Sandor in the face, but the blow had no impact on Sandor, who was holding Eddy's jacket with both hands and pushing him backwards towards the cliff. "She's my girl! My girl! I'm going to kill you for this!"

As Eddy struggled to break away from Sandor's grasp, he was being pushed closer and closer to the edge of the cliff. He tried to dig his heels in, but Sandor was too strong for him. He felt himself start to slip backwards over the edge and he grabbed onto Sandor's jacket for support.

Reiko screamed and ran over and started pulling on Sandor's arm. "Don't do this! He's the one who saved my life!"

When Sandor heard that, he took one hand off Eddy and turned to Reiko. "Saved your life? What the hell are you talking about?"

"Don't hurt him. Please let him go!"

Eddy was able to take advantage of Sandor's distraction and he yanked himself out of Sandor's grip. He reached down and grabbed a rock and smashed it into the back of Sandor's head. Sandor yelled out in pain and sank to the floor while Eddy ran towards his car.

Sandor got to his feet and made a tentative attempt to run after him but Reiko called out, "Let him go! He didn't do anything wrong!" Sandor turned back towards Reiko as Eddy got in his car and sped off.

Sandor walked back to Reiko and pointed a finger at her. "Who is he? Why did you come out here with him?"

"You could have killed him!"

"He had his hands on you. I thought I could trust you!"

"What are you doing out here? Did you follow me?"

"Yes! Yes, I did. And what were *you* doing out here with *him*? What is this place, with all the candles and flowers?"

"No, after what you did, I can't stay here with you. Please take me home."

"Not until you help me understand about all of this."

So Reiko gathered herself and told him what she remembered about the bus crash and everything that led to her being taken here by Eddy tonight.

As he listened, Sandor touched the gash in his head where Eddy had hit him with the rock. Blood was smeared across the side of his neck and made a dark stain where it was dripping onto his shirt. And when Reiko was finished, he stood there with his blood stained hands clasped in front of him like a like child begging his mother for absolution. Sandor could only look at her and ask for her forgiveness. Ask her to try to understand that he couldn't stand the thought of losing her.

"Jeff, I'm sorry. I just don't know what to say to you now, after what just happened. We can talk tomorrow. Now, please take me home." And Reiko started to walk towards the car.

Sandor grabbed her by the arm as she walked past him and pulled her back close to him. Reiko tried to push him away but he drew her nearer and kissed her passionately. "I want you."

"Stop! Don't do this!"

Sandor started to pull at Reiko's clothing. "You're not running out on me. Not after all this time."

"What are you doing? I don't want to."

"Come on, you know you always want to with me."

"Not here, not here!"

"I need you now!" and Sandor kissed her again and pulled her down to the ground. Reiko resisted but soon she was overcome by the same overwhelming surge of emotion that enveloped them the countless other times they had made love, and she surrendered to him there on the ground among the flowers and flickering candles left in memory of the dead.

And afterwards, as they lay in the grass, Reiko cradled Sandor's head in her arms and was so distressed by the feeling that her life was spinning out of control, that she didn't notice his head had not only stopped bleeding, but the wound had already completely healed.

Chapter 26

The Run On Inn was the oldest bar in the oldest neighborhood in Spokane, Washington. Joey, the bartender, used to joke that the only place in the joint that still had room for someone to carve their initials was the top of his bald head, and that's why he always wore a Mariners baseball cap.

It was 3:30 on a Tuesday morning, and as Joey straightened up behind the bar, he stared at the only person left in the place. "Come on, give me a break, Petey! I gotta close up! Some people actually *like* to go home and get some sleep."

Pete Johansson stared down at his drink. "Sleep, yeah, I remember what that used to be like. I know I'm busting you, Joey, but just one more, then I'll go home. I promise."

Joey groaned to himself but walked over to Pete and poured him a shot. "Look, Pete, you know you're one big pain in the ass to me, *right*, but I'm worried about you. You used to come in here one, two nights a week, have a few rounds, shoot the breeze and be outa here at some sort of normal hour. But now, it seems like you're living here. It's all I can do to get you outa here at night, so I can go home. What's eatin' at you? Maybe it'd be better if you talked about it."

"Since when you turn into the parish priest?"

"Well, screw you too!" And Joey started to wipe down the bar next to Pete.

"Sorry, Joey… I mean thanks for asking. But you're right I gotta go home and try to get some sleep." Pete walked out into the deserted working class streets, pulled up the collar of his jacket to take what little protection it offered against the ever-present Spokane drizzle, and started the two-block walk to his apartment.

Pete lived one flight above a discount bakery that sold day -old breads and cakes. When he moved into his room two years ago, he smiled at the irony, thinking what a perfect metaphor for himself. Past his prime and only appealing to someone willing to compromise their standards. But as he trudged up the long flight of stairs to his apartment, all he could think about was his hopes that tonight would be different than the last two weeks.

Even after two years, Pete still got the feeling that he had walked into someone else's apartment when he opened his door. The tenant before him had skipped out in the middle of the night after going five months without paying his rent, and left behind most of his meager furnishings. The landlord sought to make up some of her lost income by jacking up the rent and offering the room as "fully furnished." Since, by then, Pete's only possessions were the clothes he could shove into a large duffel bag, his trumpet and a small collection of jazz LPs, a furnished apartment seemed just fine to him. He couldn't stand the thought of using someone else's sheets or towels, but after he replaced those, he added nothing of his own.

Pete hung his damp jacket on the doorknob and pulled open the beat up convertible sofa. He shook out his pillow that he found laying on the bare floor and put it on the bed. He smoothed out his sheet and, fully clothed, sat down on the part of the mattress where the springs protruded the least. He was so exhausted that his eyes felt like smoldering coals, but he still didn't want to risk falling asleep.

Pete reached for the row of LPs propped up against the wall near his bed and grabbed the first one, a Miles Davis on Blue Note recorded in the 1950's. He'd listened to it so many times that the grooves were nearly gone, the shiny blackness now dull, almost gray. Pete didn't have a turntable anymore, but he had heard the albums so often, that just looking at the black- and- white photo of Miles playing the trumpet on the cover would cause all the tunes and the solos to come swirling back to him.

He looked down at his trumpet case and tried to remember the last time he'd opened it and taken out the trumpet to play. It was so long ago that he'd actually be afraid to try it now. His lip was so out of shape, it would take months of practice to get him back to the point where he could play a paying gig again; that is, if anyone who knew about his reputation would be willing to hire him anyway. His career was only one of the things his drinking had taken away from him.

But as much as he tried to distract himself, he couldn't keep his head up anymore. He lay down and, despite his efforts, his eyes closed almost immediately. He fell into a deep sleep and soon the images were flooding over him. The same images he had been dreaming every night for the past month.

He was swimming underwater, frantically trying to reach the surface before his breath gave out, but no matter how fast he swam he couldn't break through to the top. His lungs were about to burst, when he saw his brother Cal's hand, the hand with the rocking horse tattoo, reach out to him. Pete managed to grab the outstretched hand and was pulled to safety. He lay on the ground panting until he realized he was near the top of a cliff. He started to slide towards the edge. He clawed at the earth but he kept moving closer to the edge. He managed to grab onto a small shrub but he pulled it out of the ground and went rolling off the cliff. He was falling face down, screaming as the ground came rushing up towards him. Everything went black and then he was standing in a white room looking at someone in bed wrapped in bandages. The young man in bed didn't speak or move. Then Pete felt a hand on his shoulder and turned to see his brother, Cal.

"He needs you, Pete. You must help him get well. Tommy needs you."

"Where is he and what can I do?"

"Find my son. Stay with him and when he opens his eyes tell him he will endure. His task is just beginning."

Pete turned to look at Tommy and when he looked back at his brother, Cal was gone.

Pete opened his eyes and stared up at the ceiling. His pillow was drenched with sweat and his head was pounding. Sunlight was peering through his windows, so even though it felt like he had only been asleep for a few minutes; he knew he'd been out for hours. He pushed himself off the bed, opened the window, and let the cool air hit his flushed face. He stood there, staring at the seagulls swooping down over the trash bins behind the supermarket across the street. Two words kept going through his mind: "find Tommy...find Tommy." And now Pete realized that he might never have another normal night's sleep unless he did.

Lucinda had just finished a mystery novel and was about to take another walk to the vending machine in the corridor of the hospital. She'd lost count of the number of books she'd read in the five months she'd been sitting next to Tommy's bed. And the frustration, boredom and heartbreak of sitting in that hospital room waiting for any sign of improvement from her son had caused her to eat so many candy bars and bags of chips that she was afraid to look at herself when she passed a mirror.

When Lucinda reached for her purse she was startled to see a man standing in the doorway staring at Tommy. He didn't seem to even notice that Lucinda was also in the room. As she looked at the man she felt her heart start to beat faster. Lucinda knew she had never seen him before, but there was something about him that seemed very familiar. He took a few steps into the room and she saw the rocking horse tattoo on his hand and then she understood. "Come in, you must be Pete."

Pete walked past Lucinda and came up close to Tommy's bed. He bent over Tommy and spoke to him in a voice too soft for Lucinda to hear. "Your father sent me here to tell you everything will be alright." Then he lightly touched Tommy's arm and a low moan came from Tommy. It was the first sound Lucinda had heard Tommy make in the five months he had been in the hospital.

There were so many questions Lucinda wanted to ask Pete, but he asked one first. "How did you know it was me?"

"Cal told me about you and how you both got the rocking horse tattoo on your hands as a remembrance of your father."

"He was a good man. Better than Cal or me turned out to be."

"But how did you know about Tommy being in the hospital?"

"That was easy enough. I just Googled the name 'Tommy Johansson' in the computer at my neighborhood library. It came up with an article from a paper outside of Seattle. Local high school basketball hero injured in a bus crash. Mentioned which hospital he'd been taken to."

"I can understand that but what I meant was how did you *know* that Tommy was hurt?"

"Look, I really don't know how to explain this so it makes any sense, but Cal told me."

"Now wait a minute, Pete. What're you talking about? Ten years ago the police told me he had died. You mean they were wrong? He's still alive?"

"No, that's the thing. He's dead, I know he is. But, well, let me just come right out and say it. Cal came to me in a dream and told me Tommy was hurt and I had to find him. That's the only way he's going to get better."

"A dream! A vision in a dream… I wish I could believe in that kind of thing, but I don't."

"Neither did I. But look, here we are together in Tommy's hospital room. You can't argue with that. And now, if you don't mind, please, you've got to let me stay and finish the job."

"The job?"

"Helping Tommy get better and telling him his dad said his task is just beginning."

Lucinda didn't know what to make of Pete's story about his dream and she certainly held no faith that Pete's presence would have any effect on Tommy. When she got to the hospital the next two mornings, Pete was already there, sitting by the bed and holding Tommy's hand and softly talking to him. She hadn't noticed any real changes in Tommy, but she was happy to have Pete's company during the long hours she sat with her son each day. Even though she had never met him before, his looks and mannerisms were frequent reminders of Cal, so he felt strangely familiar to her.

They both seemed to be trying their best to avoid talking about the past, and the things that had gone wrong for both of them. But on the third night, sitting in a nearly deserted coffee shop around the corner from the hospital, they came to feel they trusted each other enough to talk about the things in their lives that had brought them to this point.

"Cal used to tell me about your father. Said even though he was only six years old when he last saw him, he had the greatest effect on shaping his life."

"Yeah, that sounds like Cal. Always making those big dramatic statements. Well, I suppose, he was right. I think both Cal and me would've turned out to be different people if it wasn't for our dad."

"I know Cal spent his life trying to live up to his father…the chaplain who loses his life in the war while trying to comfort others. It's a hard act to follow."

"Don't remind me. Do you know how many times Cal told me, 'Remember what Dad told us, it's our job to help others when they need help the most.' Just try and live up to that! And when I got into jazz and the trumpet, it made me feel selfish and guilty. Like any success I had was at the expense of some poor unfortunates that I should be helping out."

"Pete, as far as I'm concerned, Cal lost his life trying to be like his father. He felt he had to prove how good a person he could be, do something special his father would be proud of."

"You know, Cal and I went our separate ways after we both moved out of the house. I hadn't heard from him in years. Didn't even know he'd been living with you and I damn sure didn't know he had a son. Then from out of nowhere I get a phone call from him. Don't know how he got my number. He told me he finally had found his calling. He told me he was doing Dad's work and that for the first time he really felt worthwhile. I asked him what he was into, but he told me to come back to Seattle and he would introduce me to this group he was working with. Said I had to be there to appreciate it. Well, I was leaving on a tour with my band and I never got back to him. When I finally tried to contact him, it was too late. His phone was disconnected and that was that. Until…"

"Until?"

"Until those dreams. Then I made some calls and found out he had died years ago. Drugs, they told me."

"So, I suppose you never found out what *really* happened to your brother."

'Please, if you can, tell me."

"It was drugs, but maybe not for the reasons you might think. He found out about a group of Viet Nam vets who never really readjusted after the war. Most of them had long term problems with drugs. They were in a support group but it didn't seem to help them get back on their feet. Cal had the idea that he could help them."

"Was he some sort of counselor or social worker?"

"No, but that didn't stop him. He would wait for them after they got out of their meeting and tell them he wanted to help them. That if they put their faith in themselves and *him* , together through the power of the universe, or some hooey or other like that, they could beat their drug problem and get a new start on life."

"Did it work? Did they actually fall for that?"

"Would you? So he got desperate. He felt he was failing them. He had to do something to make them feel that he really understood their problems and would do anything to help them. So, he started to take drugs also."

"Oh my God, how was that supposed to do any good?"

"I couldn't reason with him. I pleaded with him. Wasn't having Tommy and me enough to give him some purpose in life? But he kept on saying that only one from among them could lead them from their travails. Travails! Who says *travails* any more?"

"What finally happened?"

"Tommy was old enough to notice his father acting strange around the house. Then Cal started inviting over some of the old vets, and, well, things got so out of hand that I had to ask him to leave. We were never really married, you know. I hoped he'd be able to straighten himself out, but he just drifted away."

"Oh, I am so sorry for you! That must've been hell for you *and Tommy*, to go through."

"And the last thing he said before he left was, 'I really don't have a choice. My father would've wanted it this way.'"

By the time they were finished talking they were the only customers left in the coffee shop. Pete paid and they stepped out into the cool breeze of the San Jose evening.

Pete put his hand on Lucinda's shoulder, "I know I can't make up for the things my brother did, but I know if it was me, I never would've left you and Tommy."

Lucinda looked at the gentle expression on Pete's face and it reminded her of Cal when she first met him. "Having you here these past few days has been really good for me. I feel like I've been alone for a very long time."

"I'm glad you feel that way. And you can count on me being here until Tommy walks out of that hospital."

And they stood on the corner and ignored the people who had now formed a line behind them waiting for the next city bus to arrive. They looked at each other and didn't know what to say next. Pete ended the silence by saying, "Well, I guess it's getting late. I'd better let you get home."

"You know, Pete, I've never thought of asking you where you're staying here in San Jose."

"To tell you the truth, I've been sleeping in the hospital visitors lounge. It's open all night and they haven't bothered me about it yet. I wash up and change over there also. I made friends with this old fella who works in information and he keeps my bag over there for me."

"Oh, Pete, you should have told me! I can't let you keep on doing that. I've got room for you over at the apartment I've been leasing since I've been here. It's got a pullout couch."

"Thanks, but I can't be putting you out like that."

"No, Pete, I really mean it. I want you to come home with me."

At 2:30 that morning, Lucinda stood in the doorway to her living room and stared at Pete. He was so insistent about not wanting to inconvenience her that he wouldn't even let her pull open the sofa bed. He slept lying on his side with his long legs pulled up so he could fit on the couch which was a good foot too short for him.

Here, in the dark room lit only by the street lamp outside the window, Lucinda couldn't help thinking how much Pete reminded her of his brother Cal. And the rocking horse tattoo on his hand made the resemblance that much more striking. Lucinda could see how easily Tommy could have mistakenly thought it was his father who saved him from drowning, instead of Pete. But twice in the past days, Lucinda had asked Pete about that day in the park, and each time Pete professed no knowledge of what happened. If it was Pete, why would he lie about being there? And if it wasn't him, then who was it?

When Lucinda and Pete returned to the hospital room at nine the next morning, they found Josanda Alvarez holding Tommy's hand. Lucinda was touched by the attentive and dedicated care that the nurse always gave her son. The look of concern on her face would make a passerby think she was a close relative, not a nurse. Lucinda sometimes fantasized about her son finally waking from his long sleep and becoming embarrassed when he saw the young, beautiful woman who had cared for him all these months.

When Josanda noticed them in the room she motioned for them to walk over to his bed. "He was really restless last night. I've never seen him try to move so much. He was jerking his arms and twitching his legs. It looked like he might have been having a dream. And this morning, he's been moaning and making these sounds, almost makes you think he was actually trying to say something."

"What did the doctor say about my son?"

"Well, he said there's nothing to worry about, and that maybe all this doesn't really indicate anything. But, when someone's been in a coma for this long, *any* signs of changes in behavior could possibly be encouraging."

"Lucinda and I will be here all day again, so if we see any changes we'll get your attention right away."

"Good, keep a good eye on him for me, I'll be back soon as I finish my other rounds."

After Josanda Alvarez left the room, Lucinda sat in her usual seat near Tommy and held his hand. She felt the pressure of his hand as he gripped hers, but this had been happening for the past two months. Pete moved to the other side of the bed and put his hand on Tommy's shoulder and leaned over so close to him that he could feel Tommy's hot breath on his face. The scars on Tommy's face had healed months ago and his normally light complexion was even paler after all this time in the hospital. Tommy's eyes were closed as usual. There was a small network of veins that appeared through the thin skin around them, but if you watched closely, you could see a small fluttering of the eyelids.

Although it would have been impossible for anyone watching Tommy to realize this, visions had started to appear in his mind. He was holding hands with Reiko and they were walking down a path in a densely wooded forest. They came to an opening in the woods and saw a circle of huts. People appeared in the clearing and bowed their heads when they saw Tommy and Reiko approaching. And then the images stopped and Tommy heard Pete's voice from someplace far away.

Pete began to say the same things he had been saying for the past three days. "Tommy, it's your Uncle Pete. I'm here with your mom. We're here to help you get better. Your mom misses you, Tommy. She wants you back. Come back to her."

Lucinda noticed that Tommy had begun to sweat and she gently wiped his forehead as Pete continued to talk to him. "Tommy, I know you don't know me and I'm really sorry I never got to see you when you were growing up, but do you know why I'm here? Do you know who sent me? It was your dad, Tommy. My brother Cal told me to come here to help you get better. He came to me in a dream. Can you believe that? Your dad sent me."

And Tommy opened his eyes.

Pete was so surprised by this that he nearly staggered backwards. Tears formed in Lucinda's eyes as she ran around to the other side of the bed and hugged Pete. "Oh my God, Pete! It's happening. I can't believe it. This is so wonderful."

Five minutes later, Tommy's doctor was talking to Lucinda and Pete as he examined Tommy. "See, see, I told you to have some faith. This is amazing, but it's only a first step. He's not focusing at all and I still have no idea what he's aware of, but from this point on, we can only hope more improvements will start to develop."

While the doctor made entries on Tommy's chart, Lucinda and Pete moved closer to Tommy's bed. Lucinda stared at him and wondered at the brightness of his blue eyes after all he had been through. And then Tommy started to move his mouth and make small sounds. The doctor quickly put down the chart as Lucinda grabbed Tommy's hand and stared into his unseeing eyes. Tommy continued to make barely audible sounds and Pete bent down over Tommy and put an ear to his mouth. The sounds became louder and sounded more like indistinct words. Lucinda touched Tommy's face. "Yes, Tommy, It's Mom. I can hear you. Talk to me."

And then Tommy blinked and stared into his mother's face and said in a voice clear enough for everyone around his bed to understand, "Reiko! Where's Reiko?"

A month later, with the aid of a cane, Tommy was walking down the hall with Nurse Alvarez. His casts had been taken off while he had still been in a coma, but after months of disuse, his leg muscles needed to be strengthened.

"So, are you sure that Reiko didn't recognize me?"

"Well, she claimed not to know who you were, but I'm sure that was only because of the trauma from that terrible accident. Deep down inside, I do believe she knew you very well."

"Maybe she acted that way because she didn't want to let her father and uncle know what happened between us."

"Happened between you? You know, you've never been too clear about just *what did* happen between you and that girl."

"No, no, it's not what you're thinking. But when we met we both knew right away there was a special connection between us, that we were important to one another. That's why I can't believe she didn't remember me."

"Now if that bus accident was bad enough to send you into a coma for five months, don't you believe that she could have gotten temporary amnesia from the same experience?"

"I know, that's what everyone tells me, but I just can't believe she didn't remember me when she saw me."

"I do believe this is where we started this conversation, so I'm not answering any more of your questions. But I have one for you. You'll be well enough to be released soon. What then?"

"You know the answer to that. I'm going to the college at San Jose to find Reiko."

"That's good, Tommy, look for her. I don't think you'll be disappointed."

But in her heart, Josanda Alvarez didn't know if that was what she really wanted to tell him.

Chapter 27

Reiko's father looked at the street map and tried to find Prince Street. He stood on a corner of the busy Japanese business district in Vancouver and let the hundreds of animated shoppers brush past him while he looked for the red circle Reiko's uncle had drawn on the map to help him locate the shop he was looking for. He tried to concentrate on the map he held in front of him, but his mind kept returning to thoughts of his wife, and his son who was now managing the family farm in Japan.

He had intended to return to Japan when Reiko left the hospital and had enrolled in college, but when Reiko's uncle had offered him a position with his company in Vancouver, he felt compelled to accept it so he could remain closer to Reiko.

His wife's health no longer seemed to be a matter for concern and she encouraged him to stay longer. His son had tried to reassure him that he would be able to handle the increased responsibility at the farm. He had even teased that he was getting twice as much work done now that he didn't have to listen to his father's endless lecturing on traditional farming techniques. Reiko's father had grumbled back that he was staying longer because he was afraid to come home and see how, in six months, his son had destroyed the farm that had been in his family for seven generations. But Reiko's father greatly appreciated the permission his son gave him to remain in Vancouver. He knew he could not return to Japan because he had an inner feeling that told him Reiko would need his help again in the future.

A mindless woman scurried by him carrying a squirming carp wrapped in such a small piece of wax paper that its thrashing tail brushed against Reiko's father, jolting him from his thoughts. He stopped another passerby and asked directions to the shop indicated on his map and reluctantly walked off towards that street.

If Reiko's father had known the true nature of his brother-in-law's home furnishing business he probably would not have accepted his offer of a job. He was first taken to the warehouse, shown a huge pile of carpets and assigned the task of removing labels which read "Made in Bangladesh" and replacing them with "Handcrafted in Tibet" labels. When he realized that the reason for the change of labels was to fool shoppers into thinking they were buying a superior and much more expensive carpet, Reiko's father refused to continue this work that he felt brought shame to his family, along with untold bad luck.

His brother-in-law laughed at him and said he had much to learn about life now that he was no longer a poor farmer. "If helping my business prosper is not one of your earthly concerns, then perhaps cleanliness is. We have enough brooms and mops, and floors and shelves that need cleaning, to satisfy your desire to do more noble work." And so Reiko's father came to work each day and sought out the dust and grime in the showroom and warehouse, much like he sought out the weevil on his farm. And like in those days back in Japan, his body absently performed the tasks at hand, while he filled his head with the songs and scriptures of the gods.

Then one day, after months of this cleaning, he saw his brother-in-law yelling at one of his employees. The man appeared to be refusing to carry out orders he was being given. Reiko's father could hear him saying something about not wanting to go back to someplace again. His brother-in-law called him a coward and a fool and told him to get out and never return to the store again. Then he called over Reiko's father and told him he had a new job for him.

"You have shown such excellence and dedication to your work, that I now know I can trust you with a position of great importance, not only to me, but to a good portion of the Japanese community in Vancouver. The man I just threw out of here could not do a simple task, going to a neighborhood business and collecting an envelope to bring back to me. This map will tell you where to go."

Finally, Reiko's father found the address he had been seeking, a shop selling silk purses and scarves embroidered with patterns of flowers and women dressed in traditional Japanese kimonos. It appeared to be only one such shop out of many similar ones on this block. The store seemed deserted when Reiko's father entered, but wind chimes rustled as the door of the shop closed and a pleasant looking older woman came from behind a beaded curtain to greet him.

The woman smiled and asked if he was there to buy a present and might she be of service in helping him select something appropriate. When he thanked her, but said he was really here to collect an envelope for his brother-in-law, Mr. Otuso, the woman's face took on a harsh look and she abruptly turned and went back behind the beaded curtain. Reiko's father could hear the woman talking to someone and then the angry voice of a man was heard arguing with her. A minute later, the woman came back out, quickly shoved a large manila envelope in his hands and, in an agitated tone of voice, told him to leave the store at once.

Reiko's father bowed and turned towards the door, but as he was about to leave he heard someone rushing out from behind the beaded curtain. He spun around to see a large man running towards him with a club in his hand.

The man swung the club at the head of Reiko's father but in one graceful motion he stepped out of the path of the blow, grabbed the man's other arm and twisted it and, with the force of his knee in the man's back, pushed him to the floor. Reiko's father bowed once again at the startled woman, who was trying to help the man up from the floor. And then he left the store with the manila envelope, as the wind chimes rustled behind him once again.

A half-hour later, when Reiko's father handed the envelope to his brother-in-law and told him what had happened in the shop, he was greeted with a hearty laugh and a slap on the back.

"I knew I could count on you to not disappoint me. Tell me, did you look in the envelope? No, a man of your honor would never open a sealed envelope that did not belong to him. Here, let me show you what you brought to me."

Reiko's brother-in-law tore open the envelope and pulled out a large amount of brightly colored Canadian money. He held up the bills and gently shook them in front of him. "You see, everyone is only too happy to borrow money from me to start their business here in Vancouver. But when it is time to pay it back, with, of course, the proper interest that is due to me, then they complain they can not afford it, that my rates are too high. Did I force them to take my money? No! But they must learn that I can force them to pay it back."

"So you send *me*, so I can be attacked by these poor, unfortunate shopkeepers."

"Ah, I had no worry of your safety. Reiko has told me many times of your exploits as a martial arts master before you grew older and came back to work the family farm."

"My safety is not the matter here. As you rightly observed before, my honor is what is of importance to me. And that is why I cannot be used by you as an object of fear over struggling workers."

"I do not have the luxury of being able to hold *my* honor to such exalted standards, but I will respect yours, if you wish. So, tomorrow you may return again to your mops and brooms and continue your task of elevating the dust off my shelves."

Chapter 28

Two days later, Reiko was sitting in the apartment her uncle had rented for her only a block off campus. She reread the letter she had just finished writing to her father and wondered if it would cause him too much concern. As much as she coveted his support, she didn't want him to leave Vancouver and return to San Jose. This was the first time in her life she was living without the supervision of a family member, and she desperately wanted to maintain her independence. Still, the events of the other night had so unsettled her that she needed to communicate with him.

She hadn't been able to put Jeff's display of violent behavior out of her mind. Reiko knew he could be jealous, but his actions were so far out of proportion to the situation that she was truly frightened of what the future might hold. As hard as it was to believe that Jeff would have actually pushed Eddy off the cliff, she couldn't deny to herself that it appeared he was about to do just that until she intervened.

Reiko could not deny, nor resist, her physical attraction to Jeff. But there was another powerful element she also couldn't deny. In his attentiveness, his desire to protect her, in his focused determination to do what was best for her, despite this at times being at odds with her own desires…yes, he did remind her all too well of her father. This compelling nature of their relationship she did not like to dwell on.

And weighing on her mind above all things was one matter…was Jeff the reason she had been protected from perishing in the burning barn on her farm in Japan when she was a child, and then again, only months ago, in a horrible crash on the highway in California? Was this the task that had been obliged of her…to save this compelling but troubled man from doing harm to himself and others?

Images of what had happened on the cliff after Eddy ran away refused to fade from her mind. At first, she thought of it as a case of Jeff forcing her to his will, laying on the ground, near the side of the highway, their love making exposed to any passing cars that might have spotted them in their headlights. But after her initial resistance, Reiko knew that she herself had given in to the moment. She had committed an act that she once would have thought unthinkable. And this loss of control of the good judgment she had always prided herself on, that was her greater concern. Was this too a manifestation of the fact that her destiny was bound to his, regardless of his actions?

So, although she did not reveal the very disturbing events of that night, writing the letter to her father helped clarify her feelings in her own mind. She remembered her original intention of achieving a grade average high enough to enable her to transfer to a superior college next fall. San Jose State was adequate, but she and her family demanded more than that for her. She made a promise to rededicate herself to that resolve. And after her harrowing experience last night, Reiko felt that leaving to go to another college would prove whether her relationship with Jeff was ordained to endure.

Reiko took the completed letter, left her apartment and walked to the mailbox on the corner. She pulled open the letter shoot but hesitated before dropping the letter into the box. Should she have revealed more of her feelings of doubt? But she knew if she told her father of the violent side of Jeff's nature her father would come to San Jose and try to force her to make a decision she was not yet prepared to make, perhaps that was not even within her own power to make. These uncertainties flooded Reiko's mind as she dropped the letter into the gaping mouth of the dark blue mailbox.

Nearly a week had passed before Reiko heard from Jeff again. He called her and spoke in an excited, upbeat manner that betrayed nothing of that night out on the edge of the cliff.

"Reiko, hey, sorry I haven't called in a while, but busy studying for finals. You too, I bet."

"Yes, Jeff, I understand. I'm preparing for my math test right now."

"Well, I bet you could use a break from all that studying, right? I want you to meet me down at the NightOwl in half an hour."

"Jeff, I can't. I need to study more tonight…maybe tomorrow."

"No, no, it's got to be tonight. I've got a surprise for you. Come on, Reiko, you're not going to ruin things are you?"

As much as Reiko didn't want to see Jeff at this moment, she also didn't want to antagonize him. If she *did* ever come to feel that events between them had become so tumultuous that it was no longer possible for her to continue with him, it would have to be gradually. "Let him down slowly" was a saying she had learned in California and with Jeff's unpredictable temper she felt that would be the best way to handle him. "Alright, Jeff, I will meet you there, but I can only stay for a short while."

"I knew you'd come, and don't worry, you won't be disappointed. See you soon."

It only took Reiko ten minutes to walk to the NightOwl. When she walked into the darkened room she saw Jeff standing at the crowded bar with his back to her. She walked up behind him and called his name. When he heard her voice, he spun around and faced her with a big smile on his face, "Hey babe, so glad you could make it. Look who's here to see you."

And the man standing next to Jeff turned around so she could see his face. It was Eddy.

Reiko blinked twice and shook her head as though she couldn't believe what she was seeing.

"See, see, I told you you'd be surprised. Look, Eddy and I are buddies now. See, no harm done the other night. Isn't that right, Eddy?"

Eddy threw his arm around Jeff. "That's right, Reiko. I should've known better than to go driving around with some other guy's girl late at night. I deserved a beating. But maybe next time I'll be kicking Jeff's ass." And Eddy tried to grab Jeff in a headlock but Jeff sidestepped him and they ended up wrestling with each other at the bar, as the other patrons moved away from them.

Jeff turned towards Reiko and saw her standing ten feet away from the bar with her hand over her mouth and a bewildered look in her eyes. "Don't worry, Reiko, if one of us gets hurt you can always use your *magic hands* on us, right. Yeah, Eddy, my girl's a natural-born healer. How about that!"

And as they laughed in camaraderie and continued to push each other at the bar, Reiko suddenly felt a sick feeling in the pit of her stomach. There was something very wrong with all of this. Something she should have realized long before.

Jeff and Eddy were so involved in their horseplay that they didn't notice Reiko running out of the bar. When Jeff realized she was gone, he ran out to the street but she was already down at the end of the next block. "That little… Wait here, Eddy, I'm going to drag her back here!"

"Aah, come on, Jeff. Don't get so upset."

"Nobody runs out on me. You'd better understand that."

"Hey, she's a girl. No sense of humor. What can you expect? Let her go and let's get another drink!"

"Okay, maybe you're right. Yeah…yeah, what can you expect from some dumb girl? Yeah, let's go in for another drink. What do you say?"

But just as he was about to walk back into the NightOwl, Jeff picked up a trash barrel and threw it across the parking lot. "Don't you worry; I'm going to teach her a lesson about manners. You can bet on that."

As Eddy followed Jeff back into the NightOwl he realized that he had probably done something very stupid in believing he could trust Jeff after what had happened on the cliff the other night. But it was a risk he'd have to take if he was going to follow his orders and stay close to Reiko until the time was right.

Chapter 29

Tommy was glad the afternoon bus to San Jose State University was half-empty. He was able to find a seat on the aisle so he could stretch out his stiff right leg in front of him. His mother and Uncle Pete had pleaded with him to let them drive him, but he felt that he had spent more than enough time dependent upon the help of others. This was a trip he had to make on his own, if only to prove to himself that he was finally able to put the months in the hospital behind him and set out to accomplish what was most important to him, finding Reiko.

Tommy got off at the main gate to the college and followed the signs to the registrar's office. The campus seemed strangely empty as he walked along the path leading to the registrar. When he arrived there, he found a row of desks attended by people working intently on computers. He cleared his throat to get someone's attention and an older man working at the desk closest to him responded without looking up from his screen. "We're busy in here, can I help you?"

"Yes, you can. I'm looking for one of your students. I'd like to know if you can help me find her. Her name is Reiko and she's a freshman."

"And how are you related?"

"Oh, we're not related, we're just good friends."

"Well, in that case we can't help you. You *have* heard of confidentiality regulations? We just can't give out personal information to just *anyone* who walks in off the streets."

"I know, but you don't understand. I've just spent nearly six months in a hospital waiting to be well enough to see her again. I didn't have her phone number or even know where to begin to look on the campus." Tommy's right leg started to tremble and he had to hold onto the counter in front of him for support. He broke out into a sweat and wiped his forehead with his hand.

The man saw his distress, walked over to him, handed him a tissue and motioned for Tommy to sit next to his desk. "Your story doesn't make much sense to me, but I can see how much this means to you. Look, I shouldn't be telling you even this much, but the term is over; that's why we're busy entering the final grades. There's a big freshman social this Friday night in the gym to celebrate the end of their first term here. Most of the kids go, so if you're lucky, maybe you'll find that girl over there. Just don't mention to anybody you heard about it from me."

Tommy reached out and gripped the man's hand. "Thank you. You don't know how much this means!"

Something about the warmth of Tommy's grip and the penetrating way he stared into his eyes made the man feel that yes, there *was* something very important about these two young people meeting each other again.

And as Tommy limped off the grounds of the college looking for an inexpensive hotel room to spend the next two nights until Friday, Nurse Josanda Alvarez had stepped into the empty workers' lounge at the hospital to make a phone call,. "Hello. It's me. Tommy left the hospital a while ago. He's probably down at the college by now looking for Reiko. Watch for them. And yes, I'm sure they're the ones we've been waiting for."

It had been over a month since Matt Connors or Donna had heard a word from their son. The letter Donna had received from him claiming that he was attending some unnamed college had been their last contact from Sandor. Matt couldn't be sure that Sandor hadn't phoned or written to Donna since then, but she swore she wouldn't conceal something like that from him. Was she telling the truth? With him in California and her still in Idaho, how could he judge?

Yet it had only been two days since he had heard from that damn Sheriff Dillon, still badgering him about whether he had any idea where Sandor might be, or if he possibly had come into any new information about the identity of the body they had found near Sandor's van back in Oregon; then Dillon asking him if he had any idea what the SJF pin might mean. Matt didn't have an answer to any of those questions, and if he did, Dillon would be the last person on earth he'd give them to.

So Matt could never have guessed that within the next hour he would know where Sandor was and that one of his own workers would supply him with that knowledge.

"Donna, it's me. I've got important news. I'm leaving for San Jose' State University tomorrow morning and I want you to email the most recent pictures you have of Sandor to me tonight. Do you know how to do that?"

"Of course I do, but what are you talking about? Are you telling me Sandor is at the college in San Jose? Did he contact you?"

"No, but ten minutes ago, Jorge, one of my newest landscapers comes to pick up his pay and he's wearing this button with the initials…"

"Not SJF!"

"Exactly, and when I saw it I nearly fell out of my chair. He told me his son is the first member of his family ever to go to college and he's so proud that his son sent him the button that stands for …"

"Damn it! San Jose Freshman, am I right?"

"Here's Dillon badgering me about that button and then it just shows up in my office. I've got to believe that's where Sandor is now. Email his picture to me. I'm going to that campus to find him."

Sandor looked in the mirror and liked what he saw. He had on his new sport jacket and a fresh white shirt, and the haircut he had gotten last week was beginning to fill in just the way he liked it. He knew he looked good and he knew Reiko would think so, too.

When he thought back to his destructive behavior with Eddy on the cliff and the scene he had made the other day at the NightOwl, he cringed. How could he have let himself lose control that way, especially in front of Reiko? When he ran into Eddy at the NightOwl, Eddy had been surprisingly friendly to him and he saw it as a perfect opportunity to make Reiko feel less disturbed by what had happened on the cliff. But when she saw him and Eddy together, could he really blame her for being so surprised and confused that she ran away? Besides, in reality, whether he would acknowledge this to himself or not, Sandor was so crazy about Reiko that he would rationalize just about anything she did, rather than confront the possibility that something was seriously wrong with their relationship.

So when he called Reiko and asked her to go to the freshman end-term social with him, he had really humbled himself to her. He had apologized for his jealous behavior and swore it wouldn't happen again, even though he, as he told her, "loved her like crazy!"

And when Reiko heard those words on her side of the receiver, she was the one to cringe. Yes, she was afraid he did "love her like crazy," but not in the sense of the word that Jeff meant. But she decided it would be wiser to go to the social with him anyway, as if there were no problem between them. She was going back to Vancouver to see her father and uncle during the month long break before the next term started. Reiko hoped that after being embraced by her father's love and wisdom and her Uncle's wise ways in practical matters she would feel prepared to answer the oppressive question of whether or not she could continue to envision Jeff as part of her future.

The night of the freshman social, the gymnasium of San Jose State University reverberated with the music the DJ was spinning. The volume blared and the college kids either shouted above it or used the intense noise as an excuse to dance with no need to make clever conversation. So, if an observer were to watch Reiko and the tall, handsome man dancing for most of the evening, he would have no way of knowing the extent or the intensity of their involvement.

And if an observer were determined to know more about Reiko and her friend, he would have to wait hours until they left the social and then discreetly follow them as they walked off the college campus and entered an unassuming brick building a few blocks away. And perhaps, a judgment might be made about the nature of their relationship by the amount of time that passed before one or both of them would eventually leave that building. And so, Tommy sat down on the bench at the bus stop across the street from the brick building and waited.

He dozed off and on throughout the night as he sat out on the cold bench, but at nine the next morning he was awakened abruptly by a beeping horn from a bus driver trying to alert Tommy that the morning bus had arrived. Tommy waved him off and sat there wondering if he had missed either Reiko or the young man leaving the building while he slept. But ten minutes later his question was answered, when the door of the building opened and the tall young man walked out onto the street and headed away from where Tommy sat.

Tommy waited until the man was out of sight, then crossed the street and knocked on the door of the brick building. No one answered, so he knocked more forcefully. A window shade on the ground floor was moved aside and someone peered out at the young man knocking on the door. Seconds later the front door was opened and Tommy stood there looking into the beautiful face of the girl he had been dreaming about since the day he met her on a plane over six months ago.

"Reiko, it's me, Tommy! I was sick, but I'm better now. I've come for you. Do you remember me? Please tell me that you remember!"

A veil seemed to lift from Reiko's eyes. The face of the young man who had once been only a stranger to her in a hospital bed now took on new significance. Reiko saw a vision of them sitting together on the airplane. She threw her arms around him and hugged him tight and whispered into his ear, "I remember us now, Tommy, I remember." And she took him by the hand and pulled him inside the door.

They stood in the living room and kissed and then he told her of his months in the coma and his fear that she wouldn't know him. She reached up and held his face in her hands. "My mind was clouded in the hospital, but last night when I left the college and was walking home, I felt a presence. I felt something swirling about me. When I heard the knocking on my door I felt I was being called from the beyond and then I saw you and I recognized you and I remembered what we had meant to one another, even though we had known each other for that one short night."

Reiko opened the door to her bedroom and gently led him inside. She drew him to her and they lay down on the same bed that Sandor had left not an hour before. "Please forgive me for being so blind all these months, but now I am yours, Tommy. Now I am yours."

Later, Tommy lay in bed as Reiko slept, their heads sharing the same pillow. He thought of all he had endured in the past months just so he could be exactly where he was now, lying next to her. Every fiber of his being had willed him to do this. Still, he couldn't quite understand how this could have become so important to him. He had only known Reiko for a matter of hours before the bus crash had torn them apart, yet even in that short time they had both felt that everything in their lives up to that point had prepared them for their meeting, And now that they were together again, they could only wait for signs of where their destiny would lead them. Tommy felt they had been brought together for a reason, a very important reason that he was still unable to grasp. And something told him that this reason would be revealed to them soon.

Feeling restless, Tommy carefully separated himself from Reiko's sleeping embrace and walked across the room to cool off in the morning breeze he felt coming in through the window. He glanced across the street and noticed someone sitting on the same bench where he had spent the night, talking into a cell phone. Tommy quickly averted his attention to a bird he saw swooping down onto a power line, never realizing that the person on the bench was talking to Nurse Josanda Alvarez and telling her, "Yes, it's just as we thought. They're together now. It's only a matter of time."

Earlier that morning, as Sandor was walking back to his apartment, he thought about Reiko's reactions last night. She had seemed at ease at the social, although the amount of vodka that had been sneaked into the punch bowl might have had something to do with that. But once they started to walk to her apartment she seemed oddly silent, and later, she seemed distracted during their love-making. She claimed she was tired from all the dancing and drinking of the evening, but considering her anger at him over the episodes involving Eddy this week, he wondered if she was still upset with him.

And her trip back to Vancouver to see her family had him worried.

Her father didn't want her to fly back, so he was driving down to pick her up. Sandor hated the thought of her spending the next few weeks with her father. He felt the old man never did like him and would probably try to convince Reiko to stop seeing him. Sandor wished he could talk Reiko into spending the break between terms with him, but she resisted his pleas that it would be good for them to spend the time off together skiing in Lake Tahoe. No, it seemed certain that unless something happened to change her plans, Reiko would be leaving in just a few days. And could he be positive that she'd definitely come back to San Jose? Sandor hated leaving his fate up to chance. And as he walked, he thought about what he could do to ensure things came out the way he wanted.

As he approached his apartment without any plan thought out yet, he was greeted by the sight of Antonio and Lola standing on the curb with luggage.

"Hey, Lola, look who's getting home at ten in the morning. Yeah, Jeff, I saw you and your Japanese sweetie lookin' mighty tight at the social last night. I guess you musta continued the party at *her place*. Ain't that right, Lola? The girl can't get enough of my roommate here."

"Ahh, leave him alone, Antonio. Maybe he just knows how to treat her right. You could probably learn some things from him."

"Jeff, can you believe this girl's lack of gratitude? Here I'm spending my winter break by goin' home with her to Chicago to visit her mom just to make sure her older brother doesn't try to get into her pants, and she talks to me that way."

"Antonio, do you *really* need to spread my family business all over the street?"

"You know, you two guys are way too much for me, especially with only two hours of sleep under me. I've got to get upstairs and get some rest. Have a good trip and try not to kill each other during the plane ride."

"Don't worry about that, roomie; it's hard to hide a dead body on an aero-plane. Hey, and by the way, I left a little present for you on the table... the keys to my van. If you want to take a spin while I'm outa town, go ahead. Just use it, don't *abuse* it. And don't go screwin' your sweetie on the back seat! That's my spot for Lola."

"That's it, Antonio! I'm killin' you *before* we get to the airport." Lola got into the cab that had just pulled up to the curb and yanked on his arm, smacking his head on the door of the taxi with a loud thud. "Ouch! See what happens when you date a girl from the *hood*? Stick with that classy girlfriend of yours, Jeff."

Antonio got into the cab and it started to pull away, but then it stopped and Antonio rolled down the window and called out to Jeff. "Say, I nearly forgot. You've got company waiting for you upstairs. Some woman says she hasn't heard from you in months. Looks a little too old for my taste, my man, but to each their own. Don't let your sweetie find out about her."

A wave of panic washed over Sandor as he turned towards his building and looked at the window of his second-floor apartment. Who could be up there? And then the realization hit him. That card he had sent to his mother telling her he was in college. Somehow she had managed to track him down. As he slowly walked up the flight of stairs he tried to formulate the story he would tell her.

When he opened the door to his apartment, a complete stranger was standing there. She was wearing jeans and a flannel shirt and had black hair pulled back into a bun. Sandor stared at her until she held out her hand to him and said, "Hello, I'm Sister Mary Catherine. I'm here to see Jeff."

Sandor took a step backwards towards the door, but realized that running away would be the worst thing he could do. "Jeff, oh yeah, Jeff. I'm a friend of Antonio's. I guess Jeff's not here."

"I'm afraid you just missed Antonio. He was going on a trip with his friend. Lola, if I'm correct. He told me that I could wait for Jeff until he got back here. Did Jeff ever talk to you about me? You know, he's here at this college on a scholarship from our school and we haven't heard from him since he left us."

Sandor realized he was in grave danger of being exposed. He put his hand in his back pocket, concealing the missing fingers, and tried to assume a casual air, which was never an easy thing for him to accomplish. "No, no, he never talked about anything like that to me. But you know how some people can be. They get all caught up in their studies and everything, especially their first year here."

"I can understand you thinking that way. But that just doesn't seem like the Jeff who lived with us all those years. I called the college months ago and got his phone number and this address. No matter when I called here, he never seemed to be home and he never returned any of my messages. And he never responded to any of my letters. I just came from the registrar's office to make sure his address hadn't changed. He didn't even send out a Christmas card. It's just not like him."

"Well, maybe Jeff's not coming back here today anyway. Why don't you just leave him a note that you were here to see him? I'll make sure he gets it."

"That's very nice of you…uhh, I don't think you mentioned your name."

"Billy, my name is Billy."

"Thank you for the offer, Billy, but I stopped off at the college because I'm going to a church related conference in San Francisco and the other sisters at the school are waiting to hear from me about Jeff. Antonio said I could wait as long as I wanted. And if I decided to leave before Jeff came home I could just pull the door shut behind me."

"Well, in that case, maybe I'll just leave myself and…" but before Sandor could finish his thought he was interrupted by the sound of the downstairs door slamming open and footsteps running up the staircase.

Sister Mary Catherine started to smile broadly. "Oh, that must be Jeff now. I'm in luck."

Then the door of the apartment swung open and Antonio rushed into the room. "Hey, Jeff, you and your friend are still here. Can you believe that Lola? She left the plane tickets on the table. Gotta hurry!" And he grabbed an envelope off the dining table and ran back out the door.

Sandor and Sister Mary Catherine starred at each other in silence as the downstairs door slammed shut and the cab's tires squealed as it pulled away.

"You told me your name was Billy, but Antonio called you Jeff. Just what the hell is going on here? Where *is* Jeff?"

"He was in a hurry. He must've made a mistake."

"Don't give me that! There's something funny going on here and I'm going to find out what it is."

Sister Mary Catherine moved towards the door but Sandor blocked her way. "Get out of my way, whatever your name is! I'm going back to the registrar and tell him about this and find out just what happened to Jeff."

She pushed him aside and opened the door and started down the stairs. Sandor knew he couldn't afford to let her tell her story to the registrar, not with that dead body he'd left back in Oregon. He ran down the stairs behind her and tried to grab her arm. She pulled away from him, but tripped, then screamed and tumbled headfirst down the long staircase and landed in a twisted heap at the bottom.

She had already stopped breathing by the time he reached her body.

As Sandor slowly walked backwards as he pulled Sister Mary Catherine up the long staircase to his apartment, he had time to think of what he had to do next.

When he had the body back in the apartment he rolled it over to a corner so the blood wouldn't stain the area rug, but then Sandor noticed there was only a small streak that had run out of her nose. He realized that since the injuries were internal, it wouldn't be necessary to clean up, or dispose of, any bloody evidence.

Then he went to the kitchen and got the ice pick that he was going to use to break open the padlock on the door to Antonio's room. He knew whatever he needed to carry out his plan could be found inside.

Chapter 30

While Reiko continued to sleep, Tommy had decided what needed to be done next. After finally finding Reiko, he couldn't tolerate the thought of being away from her so soon. Reiko told him her father was driving down from Vancouver to pick her up tomorrow and take her back to Canada for the month-long break before the next term.

Tommy knew that he had to convince Reiko that it was important for them to be together. He wanted to go back to Vancouver with her.

When Reiko did awake it was almost noon. She jumped from the bed and threw her arms around Tommy's neck. "Oh, Tommy, I was afraid I'd been dreaming! But you really are here, you really are."

They kissed and then Tommy held her hand and said, "There's something important I want to ask you."

"Yes, Tommy, but I have to tell you this first! I want you to come back to Vancouver with me. I don't want to be away from you. Please, would you come with me?"

A short while later, Tommy was back in his hotel room packing his few belongings. Reiko had gone off to do errands she needed to accomplish before their trip tomorrow and Tommy would be meeting her back at her apartment in a few hours. He sat on the bed that took up nearly all the space in his tiny hotel room and he thought of all the commitment and determination that had taken him from his hospital room to the point where tomorrow he would be traveling with Reiko.

But he knew he couldn't give himself the credit for all that inner strength. He remembered what his Uncle Pete had told him. His father had willed him to recover from his coma, and although his mother, and even his Uncle Pete, held no conviction that there was any sense to believing that, Tommy felt otherwise. And the time he would spend with Reiko this next month would tell him why he had been saved.

Tommy lay down on his bed, exhausted from his nearly sleepless night and the events of the past few days he had pushed his still-weakened body to endure. Tommy knew he needed to sleep for an hour before he could gather the energy to return to Reiko's apartment, but there was one thing he had to do before he fell asleep. He reached for his cell phone and punched in a number. "Hello, Mom, it's me. I'm doing great."

"Tommy! Where have you been? Why haven't you called sooner? Peter and I have been so worried about you!"

"Sorry, Mom. I've just been involved with finding Reiko and making plans. I didn't want to call you until everything was settled."

"Settled, what's settled?"

"Reiko's father is picking her up tomorrow to go back to Vancouver during the term break and I'm going with her."

"So Reiko remembered you when she saw you? And it's gotten this serious already? Does her father know you're going back with her?"

"No, not yet, but we're sure he'll understand."

"What kind of a father would understand something like that? Tommy, do you know what you're doing?"

"I've got no choice, Mom; I can't be apart from Reiko now. It's too important."

"You're not strong enough yet to be doing this now. If it's so important that you and Reiko be together then it can wait for a month until she comes back to school. Let Pete and I come and get you and bring you home so you can get your strength back. Tommy, how about that Tommy?...Tommy are you listening to me...*Tommy?*"

But Tommy's eyes were closed as the cell phone lay on the side of his bed with his mother's pleas unheard as he dropped into a deep sleep.

Sandor paced up and down in front of Reiko's apartment. She wasn't home when he got there and he'd already been waiting nearly an hour for her. He kept going over the alternatives in his mind. When the other sisters didn't hear from Sister Mary Catherine tonight and then she didn't attend the conference tomorrow, it would be clear that something had happened to her. And since the sisters *and* the college registrar knew she was looking for Jeff, it wouldn't be long before the authorities would be coming to question him. He'd have to lie convincingly about his identity to the police, and if they should send his picture to the sisters then they'd know he had assumed Jeff's identity. Sandor knew he couldn't handle the pressure; his head was already pounding. No, the risk of staying and trying to bluff his way out of it was too great. He felt he had only one choice, to run.

Still, Sandor knew that if he left without Reiko, he'd never see her again. He couldn't bear the thought of losing her, just like he lost Jeanna back in Idaho. If only he could convince her to go away with him. They could drive someplace far away and maybe she would realize how much he meant to her. She'd never have to know the truth about what happened to the real Jeff or Sister Mary Catherine. They could drive all over the country; show her what a great place it was. Just keep on moving. She could always go to college when she was older; yeah, that could always wait. If only he could convince her! And if he couldn't, then, as much as he regretted it, he knew what he would have to do.

The time dragged on and Sandor switched the bottle of wine he was carrying from hand to hand in impatience and then leaned against Antonio's car and scanned the streets in every direction looking for a sign of her. And then he saw her, still a block away, walking towards him. As she got closer he could see she was carrying clothes from the dry cleaner over one shoulder and a bag from the neighborhood drug store in the other. She seemed lost in thought and didn't notice Sandor standing on the corner as she walked up to her building and struggled to take out her keys.

"Hey, Reiko, a penny for your thoughts!"

Startled by the sound of his voice, Reiko dropped the dry cleaning she was carrying onto the street. "Jeff, you scared me! What're you doing here?"

"Here, let me help you with that. I don't know what you'd do without me." He picked her clothes up, gave her a quick kiss and motioned towards the door. "Go ahead, you can open it now."

Reiko didn't know what to make of Jeff's showing up unexpectedly, but he seemed to be in a good mood. Judging from the bottle of wine he was holding he probably wanted to have a drink goodbye before she left for Vancouver. They walked into her apartment and Sandor watched Reiko pack her freshly cleaned clothing into the luggage she had left open on her couch and put the bag from the drug store into an overnight case.

"So, I can see you're serious about going to Vancouver for a month. Have you thought over my idea of us going away together for a while and then you could go back home after that?"

"No, Jeff, no, I could not disappoint my father that way. He has been planning our trip home together for weeks."

"Sure, I understand, but we could just go away for a week and then you could spend the rest of the break with him."

"He has the trip already planned out. There would not be time enough to go away with you also."

"Then instead of him coming all the way down here to pick you up, what if I drive you up north and we meet him in Seattle? I've got Antonio's car and that would make it easier for your dad."

"I am sure that would be nice, but you do not understand Japanese parents. You can not, at the last moment, just change plans they have made. My father tells me he is going to drive me up the coastline of California and then into Oregon. He says it is very beautiful in Oregon. Maybe you know Oregon. Have you ever been there?"

"*Me... Oregon? No*, I've never been there. What makes you think I've been in *Oregon?* "

Reiko heard the change in Jeff's voice. The affability had been replaced by a suspicious tone that Reiko had been all too familiar with lately. She had tried to keep the conversation as pleasant as possible, hoping to get Jeff to leave quickly and without any problems. Tommy might be returning shortly, and she desperately wanted to prevent a confrontation between them.

"So, are you sure there's no way I can convince you to go away with me for a few days?"

"Jeff, please, I just explained it to you."

"Okay, okay, there's no harm asking, is there? So, this is what the wine's for."

"Is for what?"

"Well, as long as we're not going to see each other until next term, then call it a toast to the great time we had these past months and to picking up where we left off when you get back."

"If you want, Jeff, yes. I have enough time for your toast but then I have many things to do to get ready."

"Good, good. Just one drink, and then I'll go and leave you to your chores. That cork screw is still in the kitchen, isn't it? I'll get it."

Sandor walked into the kitchen and rummaged through the cabinet drawer until he found the corkscrew, He opened the bottle and poured the wine into two water glasses he found sitting on the counter. He turned and saw Reiko staring out the living room window, so he knew she wouldn't notice when he reached into his pocket and pulled out the two capsules he had taken from Antonio's room. He deftly broke them open and poured the fine powder into her glass. He swished it around and it dissolved at once, just as Antonio had always told him it would. And if Antonio was right again, in only a few minutes Reiko would be unconscious.

Sandor walked back to Reiko and held out the wine to her. "Not the fanciest glass in the world, but it'll serve the purpose." He held up his glass in the air waiting for Reiko to touch her glass to his. When she did he said, "To the future. May we always be together."

Reiko gulped the wine down quickly, trying to bring the goodbye to a quick end. Sandor took both their glasses and put them on the coffee table. He moved towards Reiko and she thought he was going to kiss her. She turned her cheek, but instead he took her in his arms and began to whisper into her ear. "You know I could never let anything come between us, don't you? I know I've made some mistakes, but things are going to be better, I promise you."

Reiko pushed away from him and held her hand to her temple. She started to sway on her feet and she moved to the couch and sat down. "I'm not feeling well. You should go now, Jeff."

Sandor walked over to Reiko and stroked her hair as she closed her eyes. "Don't worry; you're going to be fine. You just need to rest. Here, why don't you lie down? " And as Reiko slumped over on the couch, Sandor placed a pillow under her head and put her feet up. Then he sat on the floor in front of her, holding her limp hand and waited until she was motionless.

As Sandor waited for it to be dark, he thought about what he needed to do. Reiko had already completed her packing for the trip with her father, so all he had to do was bring her bags down to Antonio's car. Then he would pull the car into the alleyway between her house and the house next door. When it was dark enough he would carry Reiko downstairs and lay her on the back seat. The big question that Sandor hadn't answered in his own mind was what he would tell Reiko when she woke up, probably two to three hours later.

He thought of a story he could tell her to explain why she woke up in the back of Antonio's car as they were traveling away from the college. He didn't know what her reaction would be. Having somebody else in the car to confirm his story might reassure her he was telling the truth, And if she didn't believe him, he could use someone else to help him control her and try to calm her down, until he had her safely far away and could then help her see that they needed to spend their future together.

So, Sandor would need the help of someone he trusted with all of this. Sandor hadn't come to trust many people in his lifetime, but there was someone he thought of who he had come to feel saw the world much as he did. He reached for the phone in Reiko's apartment and called him.

Later that afternoon, Sandor's father stood in the middle of the campus at San Jose State University and looked at the small number of young men and women walking by and realized he must have arrived during intersession. That meant it would be even harder to locate Sandor. He knew he couldn't go to the registrar and ask where his son lived because Sandor wouldn't be using his real name. And considering what had happened in Oregon, he didn't want to do anything to attract the attention of college personnel.

So he stood there next to the entrance to the cafeteria with copies of the pictures of Sandor his ex-wife had emailed him. He held the pictures up to whoever walked in or out of the building saying, "I'm trying to find my son. Do you recognize him?" Each of the passing students either brushed past him or nodded no, until a short curly haired girl, wearing the SJF pin on her sweater, stopped and took a close look at the picture.

"So you're sure you're his dad and not some cop or guy who works for a collection agency? Nah, I can see the resemblance."

"Do you know my son? Do you have any idea where I could find him?"

"Well, I don't know where he lives, but he's in my psychology class and I know he hangs out in this place in town called the NightOwl 'cause I've seen him there a few times."

Sandor's father muttered a hurried "Thanks so very much" and started to walk off in the direction of his car when the girl called to him and he turned around to face her.

"One time my dad came looking for me and it just about saved my life. Good luck, mister. I hope you find your son today."

At six o'clock that evening, Tommy awoke with a start. From the darkened sky he saw through his window, he could tell that he had slept far too long. He called Reiko but her answering machine picked up. He nearly shouted into the phone "Reiko, it's me, Tommy! I'm sorry, I feel asleep. Don't go anywhere. I'm coming right over!"

He grabbed his bag and ran out to the street and jumped into the cab in front of the hotel. He was at Reiko's apartment in five minutes, but when he rang her bell she didn't answer. He was too late. She was gone. He looked in the window and saw no trace of Reiko, but he could see her phone on its stand next to the window and heard the insistent beep announcing the message he had left for her in the empty apartment.

Tommy stood on the corner and looked up and down the street, but saw no signs of where Reiko had gone. So he hailed a passing cab and told the driver to take him to the only place he thought he could get help.

Tommy trotted into the police station and told the desk clerk he had an emergency to report. The clerk, seeing the urgency on Tommy's face, directed him to an officer sitting across the room. Tommy started to talk to the officer before he got halfway to his desk. "Please, you've got to help me! My girlfriend is missing!"

The officer put down his coffee and motioned for Tommy to sit next to his desk. "Sorry to hear that, young fella. How long has your girlfriend been missing?"

"I'm not exactly sure, could be four or five hours by now."

"Wait a minute; four or five hours, I'd hardly call that missing."

"But she *is* missing! We had plans to go away together. Her father was going to pick us both up at her apartment. And when I got back to her place she was gone. I looked in the window and saw that her luggage wasn't there anymore."

"Uh huh, and so, just what do you think that means?"

"She wouldn't have left without me. I think somebody took her against her will!"

"So you think she's been *abducted*. Now, do you have any ideas just who might have done that to her?"

"Yes, yes, I do. I think it's her old boyfriend, His name is Jeff and he's a student at San Jose State, just like my girlfriend, Reiko."

"So, if I have this correct, you don't think your girlfriend could have *possibly* changed her mind about going away with you. And you think this guy, *Jeff*, a college student, *forced her*, in some way, to go off with him. And she's been missing all of how long? Four hours! Well, we got quite a case here."

"What's wrong with you? How can you be making some kind of joke of this?"

"Look here, young fella, first of all, since no one's actually seen any harm come to her, I can't even take a missing person report till she's been gone for a week. And secondly, well look, I feel sorry for you, I can see how upset you are, but if the police had to investigate every young girl that's run off on her boyfriend, we'd have to double the size of the force."

"So just what am I *supposed* to do now?"

"Here, I'm going to take all the information from you. And even though I can't make an official report yet, I'm going to tell my boys to keep their eyes open on this. If I hear anything at all, I'll contact you. Till then, you're on your own. Just promise me you won't do anything stupid. But, look, if I was you I wouldn't blow this all out of proportion. In all likelihood, your girlfriend will show up by herself, with an apology. Just be patient."

So for the second time since he discovered Reiko was missing, Tommy did the only thing he could think of doing. This time he took a cab back to Reiko's apartment and sat on the bench across the street hoping that the police officer was right, and she'd return home soon.

Sandor's father drove his van slowly down the street looking for the address he had convinced the bartender at the NightOwl to give him, although it would be more accurate to say the $50 he handed him did the convincing. The bartender said the boy in the picture came in a few times a week and hung out with a Japanese girl. He did most of the drinking while the girl had an occasional beer, but she seemed to be the one with more money and she ran up the tab in her name. Matt smiled at the thought of his son getting the girl to pick up the tab, but then the reality of the circumstances that brought him to San Jose brought back the grim nature of his search for his son.

As soon as the van pulled up in front of Reiko's building, Tommy got off the bench across the street. And when the driver of the van knocked on Reiko's door, Tommy crossed the street and waited for the man to walk back to his van.

"Excuse me, I saw you knocking on Reiko's door. Do you know her?"

"No, I actually don't. But I see she's not home anyway."

"So, if you don't know her, do you mind my asking just why you were knocking on her door?"

"And do you mind me just asking *you*, who are you and what's with all the questions?"

"Look, I'm sorry if I sounded rude but Reiko is my girlfriend and she was supposed to be here and she's not, so I was wondering if you knew anything about that."

"So she's *your* girlfriend. Well, let me ask you something. Does this boy look familiar to you?" Matt held up Sandor's picture and when Tommy saw the face staring out at him he grabbed the picture out of Matt's hand.

"It's him! He's the one who took Reiko! Who are you?"

"*Took her*! Took her where? He's my son. I've got to find him."

Tommy and Matt Connors stood there glaring at each other, both desperately wanting to find Sandor and not knowing even where to begin to look.

Chapter 31

As Sandor drove Antonio's van, Eddy turned around and looked at Reiko's unconscious body in the back seat. "She's still out. Just how many pills did you slip in her drink?"

"I'm not sure. I think I put in two."

"Two! For a girl her size? Is that what Antonio told you to do?"

"Tell me? No, he didn't tell me *anything*. I broke into his room and grabbed them. I knew where he kept his stash. He told me lots of stories about guys using these things on girls."

"She's been out a long time. Maybe you gave her an overdose. We should be looking for a hospital."

Don't be so worried! Antonio always said that all they do is make the girl sleep. The more you give her the more she sleeps, that's all. Besides, I thought you were here to help me out."

"Sure, sure I am. But when you called me up and asked me to go on a little trip with you and Reiko and if I could help you out with a favor along the way, I didn't expect *this*. I mean, what's the purpose of this anyway? What's it going to accomplish?"

"Well, let's just say I've got a problem, and I need some time with Reiko so I can get her to see things my way."

"Must be one hell of a problem to get you to drug her and drive way out here."

"Look, you're my buddy, right? I can trust you and you can trust me, right? I asked you to come with me in case Reiko woke up before we got to where we were going. I figured you could help me keep her calm. I mean, she seems to like you. She trusted you enough to let you drive her out to the scene of the bus accident that night I saw you both out there. So let me drive a little longer and I'll tell you all about it."

"Okay, Jeff, you can count on me. But, at least you can tell me where we're headed."

"I thought we'd just drive towards Lake Tahoe and when we saw a motel that looked sort of secluded, we'd stay there for a few days."

"A motel in Tahoe…no, I don't think that's such a good idea. We don't know how Reiko's going to be acting by the time we get there. There are always too many tourists around Tahoe. If someone saw or heard something strange, they might report it."

"Then maybe you've got a *better* idea."

"Yeah, I do. I've got a cabin out in the woods up north by Crescent City. This time of year it should be real deserted. I think it's just what we're looking for. People up there know me and I can go into town and get us provisions without anybody giving it a second thought."

"Sounds great, Eddy. I always felt it was a lucky day when I met you."

"You mean once you stopped trying to shove me off that cliff, right, buddy?"

"I'm glad you can joke about it now because I still feel bad about all that. But I'll make that up to you one day, don't you worry."

"I'll hold you to that, but for now just keep on driving and I'll tell you how to get where we're going."

Two hours later, it was turning dark and Reiko still hadn't regained consciousness. Sandor pulled off the road into a small, dusty gas station. "Eddy, while I'm filling up the van, why don't you see what kind of snacks you can get us in the shop."

Eddy bought a few bags of chips, a package of cheese sticks and three bottles of water. Then he found the men's room at the back of the station and went into the filthy little room and reached for his cell phone. He punched in a number and waited for the phone to roam for a signal. Eddy muttered, "Come on! Come on!" to himself and then he finally heard his phone connect to the number he called.

In a hushed voice, Eddy spoke into the phone. "It's me. I'm with Reiko and Jeff. I'm headed towards the Village." And then, suddenly, Sandor walked into the men's room and Eddy snapped his phone shut.

"Whoa there! You were on your cell? Who'd you be speaking to from here in the bathroom?"

"Oh, just my mom. She calls me three, four times a week. You know how they can be. Told her I was goin' to be out of town for a few days."

"Well, I think it's a good idea not to use our phones. Who knows how they can trace calls nowadays. Besides, you'd better get back to the van and keep your eye on Reiko while I use the john."

And as Eddy walked back to the van, nearly two hundred miles away, Josanda Alvarez put away her phone and turned to Tommy's mother and his uncle Pete. "Thank God for Eddy! He's headed to the Village with Reiko. But Jeff's with them. We've got to do something about that. Pete, can you drive to San Jose and pick up Tommy and drive towards the Village with him? Reiko and he should be together from this time on."

"Sure, I'll go get Tommy and if you give me a map I can find the Village. But I'm worried about what Jeff might do if he figures out what's going on."

"Don't worry, we can count on Eddy. He's one of our most reliable brothers. He'll call me again when he has more information."

With the rough map that Josanda had hastily drawn lying on the car seat next to him, Pete thought of the dramatic turn his life had taken in the past few weeks…and here he was today, driving to pick up his nephew who had been a complete stranger to him, to help him find his girlfriend and then take them to this place called the Village. And what did he know about this Village? Only that Josanda had talked with such fervor about how it was Tommy's destiny to go there with Reiko. That coupled with the insistent dream of his brother, Cal, telling him that Tommy had some sort of mission to fulfill, convinced Tommy's mother that Pete should at least take him there and let them judge for themselves what the Village had to offer them. And so he called Tommy on his cell phone to tell him he was coming.

As Matt Connors paced nervously next to him, Tommy spoke into his cell phone. "So, she's alright. He hasn't hurt her. …You're coming to get me? Where are they headed?…The Village! What's the Village?…Okay, okay, you'll be here soon and you'll tell me then…Yes, I'll be waiting at Reiko's. Just hurry!"

Sandor's father grabbed Tommy's arm, "Someone knows where my son and that girl are? Tell me!"

"Why should I tell you? Are you going to help us find them?"

"Look, in the first place, I don't know why you're making my son out to be some kind of 'bad guy.' It's that girl's own business if she wants to go away with him, isn't it?"

"She never would've left without me. He *forced* her! Now let go of my arm!"

"You're kidding yourself! Face facts, she just wanted to be with my son, not you."

"Reiko told me all about him. I *know* he must've forced her to leave with him. And if you know so much about your son, why are you walking around with a picture of him, trying to find him?"

"That's my business, not yours! But if you know where my son is, you'd better tell me or you'll be sorry!" Tommy tried to pull himself out of Sandor's father's grip but this only angered him more. He grabbed Tommy by the shirt with his other hand and started to shake him. "I'm only going to give you one more chance. Tell me where he is!"

Suddenly, his legs were kicked out from under him and he fell on the floor with a grunt. He looked up to see who had attacked him and was met with a kick in the shoulder that sent him rolling sideways. Reiko's father looked down at him. "Are you ready to talk like a man or must I keep you down on the floor like a disobedient pup?"

Sandor's father slowly pulled himself to his feet, looked at the old Japanese man standing in front of him in a martial arts position, and realized that despite his age, he had no desire to physically engage the older man. Instead, he took a few steps away and said, "Who the hell are you and what do you have to do with this?"

In the next few minutes, Tommy told all that he knew to Reiko's and Sandor's fathers. Matt Connors, without mentioning that his son was using someone else's name, told them he meant them no harm and that all he wanted to do was find his son. Thus they learned that they all had the common goal of finding the car that was now heading north towards Crescent City. And there was nothing more they could do to achieve that goal until Pete arrived.

They drove another hour and then Sandor pulled off onto a narrow side road, where there were no lights. Aside from an occasional passing car; the only light came from the full moon overhead.

"Why are you stopping? Tired? Want me to drive?"

"Yeah, I'm going to need your help, but not with driving."

Sandor slowed the van down and pulled over to the side of the road. He got out and walked to the enclosed cargo area of the van and pulled out a shovel and held it up for Eddy to see. "Come on out. We've got some work to do."

Eddy took a quick glance to see if Reiko was still sleeping and then jumped out of the van to catch up with Sandor who was walking away from the road out towards the barren landscape. By the time Eddy caught up with him, Sandor had already started to dig a hole.

"If we don't screw around, we can get this done in ten, maybe, fifteen minutes. But this ground's pretty damn dry, not so easy to dig. I'll do the first shift and when I tire out, you jump in."

"Jeff, just what the hell is this all about? Digging a hole in the middle of nowhere; are you looking for something you buried out here"?

Sandor stopping digging and looked at Eddy with a smile, "Just the opposite. We're making a deposit, not a withdrawal."

"Deposit! What's going on here? I'm getting a real bad feeling about this! What're you going to put in the hole?"

"Hey, what's with you, man? Don't get all nervous on me now. Can't you handle a little suspense? Are you in this with me or not?"

"Wait a minute, wait one fucking minute! You're not thinking of doing anything to Reiko?"

Sandor dropped the shovel and ran over to Eddy and grabbed him by his shirt. "Don't ever say anything like that again. I love her! I'd never do anything to hurt Reiko! Do you understand that?"

Eddy pulled away from Sandor's grasp. "Okay, I got it! Just don't get so damn rough. So then, tell me, what the hell *are* we digging this hole for?"

"If you just shut up, so I can start digging, you'll find out soon enough." And Sandor picked up the shovel and continued to dig. While Eddy paced back and forth, Sandor dug a hole three feet deep and then tossed the shovel to Eddy. "Do another couple of feet deeper yourself and that should be good enough."

All the digging in the hard ground caused Sandor to shake his throbbing hand, amazed that he still felt such vivid pain in fingers he no longer possessed. When Eddy was standing in the hole up to his chest, Sandor reached out his other hand, pulled him out of the hole and they walked back towards the van.

"So now I'm going to show you why we needed to dig that hole. But I want you to remember that the reason I asked you to come out here was that you were my buddy and I knew I could trust you, no matter what. I was right about that, wasn't I? I mean, if I wasn't, let me know now."

"Sure, don't worry about that, Jeff. You know you can count on me."

"Good, that's what I wanted to hear." Sandor opened the cargo compartment in the back of the van and motioned for Eddy to come over. "Take a look at this."

In the darkness of the night, it was hard for Eddy to see what Sandor was pointing to, so he leaned over to get a better look. And then he saw it. Curled up in a heap in the corner, was the body of a woman. When Eddy realized what he was looking at he jerked his head out of the cargo compartment and turned away from the van and vomited on the desert ground.

While Eddy kneeled on the ground panting and wiping his mouth, Sandor laughed at him. "Too much for you, huh? Suppose it was a little bigger surprise than you expected. I'll take care of it myself. Clean yourself off and stay here and keep an eye on Reiko. We'll talk about this later." And

Sandor walked back to the hole they had dug, dragging the body of Sister Mary Catherine behind him.

Eddy got to his feet and leaned back against the van for support. He knew why he had come with Jeff but he hadn't planned on this. He thought of Reiko and opened the back door of the van to look at her. Her eyes were still closed and he leaned over to listen to her breathing. He picked up her hand and held it in his own. Then he gently stroked her long black hair. Even after the ordeal she had been through she still looked beautiful to Eddy. It was hard for him to suppress the thought that he wanted Reiko for himself. He wished he could resolve to go off with her, convince her that she was far better off with him than with Tommy. Yet, despite his feelings for Reiko, his allegiance to the Village was even greater, and he understood that his own selfish desires were nothing compared to the importance Reiko and Tommy would have to the brotherhood of the Village.

A few minutes later, Reiko slowly opened her eyes then tried to push herself to a sitting position. As her eyes focused, she recognized who was sitting next to her. "Eddy, it's you! Why am I in this van? Where am I? Where are you taking me?"

"Don't try to sit up yet. Save your energy for later. Jeff will be back soon and it'd be better if he thinks you're still asleep."

"Jeff is here too? Where is he? My father, I was waiting for him. He will be looking for me!"

"He knows you're with me, but listen to me, we don't have much time. Jeff will be back in a few minutes. He thinks I'm here to help him..."

"Help him! Can't you see that he took me here against my will? How can you be helping him? Don't wait for him! Let's drive away before he gets back."

"That'd be nice, only he's got the keys. But don't worry, Reiko. I'm here to help you. We know it's important for you and Tommy to be together. Jeff doesn't know it, but I'm taking you to meet Tommy. It's safe there and you can stay as long as you need to."

"How do you know about Tommy and me? And what do you mean by *we know?* What is this all about, Eddy?"

"When you and Tommy were taken to the hospital at San Jose after the bus accident, Josanda Alvarez knew that you were the ones we were waiting for."

"Josanda Alvarez, the nurse from the hospital? Why was she waiting for Tommy and..." But before she could finish, Eddy put his hand to her mouth.

The sound of Sandor dragging the shovel along the hard ground made them turn and look through the back window of the van. "He saw us talking!

When he gets here don't argue with him about anything. Just go along with whatever he says."

Sandor tossed the shovel into the back of the van and walked over to Reiko. "Hey, my *sweet thing* is finally awake. You slept halfway up the coast. How're you feeling?" Sandor motioned for Eddy to get in the driver's seat and Sandor got in the back next to Reiko. He reached over and took Reiko's hand and kissed it. A chill went through her but she remembered what Eddy said and did nothing to show Sandor how she was really feeling.

"I just couldn't stand the thought of you going up to Canada with your father for the whole winter break from college. So our pal Eddy, here, was nice enough to offer us the use of his cabin up north for a few days. And don't worry, your father called on your cell while you were sleeping and I told him we were going to Crescent City and he could meet us there in a few days. He said that was fine, no problem *at all*. Isn't that right, Eddy?"

"That's right, Reiko, no problem at all."

Reiko's head spun as she tried to make some sense of what was happening, but on the outside she smiled at Sandor and said, "Yes, my father is a very understanding man. He would not mind at all."

And with Eddy now driving, they headed farther north on their way to their destination in the forest on the outskirts of Crescent City.

Chapter 32

Pete stared at the highway as he started the long drive towards Crescent City. From his seat in the front of the van, Tommy turned sideways to see Reiko's father and Matt Connors sitting uneasily next to each other in the back row.

"Look, I really don't know where you're driving me, just as long as I get to see my son."

Pete answered without taking his eyes off the road. "Damn right you don't know where you're heading and it's going to stay that way. The only reason I agreed to take you with us was because I hope you can talk some sense into your boy when we catch up to him. It would make things a lot easier that way."

Tommy turned towards Pete. "What makes you think we can trust *him* any more than we can trust his son?"

Reiko's father answered Tommy's question for him. "Because if he does not help us get my daughter away from his son I will break his back, and he knows that. Don't you, Mr. Connors?"

Matt Connors put his hand on the back of Pete's shoulder and shook him. "You'd better keep this guy away from me, or I'm not making any promises just what might happen!"

"There shouldn't be any need for trouble. You want to find your son and we want to leave with Reiko. It's as simple as that. We're here to help each other. Aren't we?"

"Yeah, sure. Just keep *him* calm and I'll help you all I can."

Tommy looked at his own reflection in the window of the passenger's door and wondered when he would receive his father's help again. It had been so long since he had seen him. But he felt that that he was soon to find out why his father had protected him in the past, soon to find out the mission he felt had been established for him. He knew that his father would not abandon him and that also meant helping him rejoin Reiko once again.

The silence in the van was broken by the ringing of a cell phone. Pete put his phone to his ear and then announced to the others, "It's Eddy and he's with Reiko and Jeff...sounds like they're about an hour ahead of us."

Tommy shouted towards Pete's phone, "Reiko, it's me, Tommy! We're coming to get you!"

Pete quickly covered the mouthpiece of his phone. "Are you crazy? We can't let Jeff know we're following them!" He quietly spoke into the receiver. "Eddy, are things okay? What about Reiko and Jeff...they left the car for a minute? ...good, yes, I know. Josanda told me that we've got to meet up with you before you get to the Village. She said if you take the long way to Crescent City, we'd have enough time to meet you at the shed by the bridge. Do you know where she meant? ...That's right, that's the one she told me about. We'll be there in less than two hours and Josanda said remember, whatever you do, don't take him to the Village."

As soon as Pete turned off his phone, Matt Connors yelled at him, "When we meet up with them, just leave my son *to me*. Don't forget that! And what's all that talk about the *Village*? Just what the hell is the Village anyway?"

Reiko's father stared at him with an icy glare. "That is not for someone such as yourself to ever understand." And the van rode on in silence once again.

Sandor helped Reiko into the back seat of the van, climbed in beside her and slammed the door shut. "That's enough driving on these back roads. Get us on a highway so at least we can find a place with a *real* bathroom the next time we need one. How much longer anyway? This trip is taking us forever."

"Sure, Jeff, we'll be hitting the highway in a few minutes. Now that it's dark there should be less cars on the road."

"Good, and turn on your wipers. It's starting to rain and I don't want to take a chance with any accidents."

Reiko spoke up for one of the few times on the trip. "Yes, please, Eddy, please drive slowly. It is so dark out here."

Eddy looked at Reiko's pale face in the rearview mirror, "Don't worry, Reiko, I wouldn't let anything happen to you. You can count on that."

Eddy drove another five minutes until he reached the entrance to the highway. The rain was coming down harder now and he slowed down and stopped to read the small markers on the road to see which ramp would take him north towards Crescent City. Eddy opened his window and peered out into the darkness at the rain- drenched sign until he saw the small arrow pointing towards the road heading north. He pulled out onto the road, thinking that he had to find a way to delay their arrival until Pete and Tommy were able to get to the shed.

They drove for ten miles in the rain and the increasing fog and then saw a large green highway sign that announced in bright reflecting letters that the Crescent City exit was only a mile ahead.

Sandor leaned over from the back seat and slapped Eddy on the arm. "That's it! You found the place for us. How much longer from here?"

"You know, it's not by the highway exit. It's more back in the woods. We've still got a ways to go yet."

"So step on it then! It feels like we've been traveling all day and night to get here. Reiko wants to get out of the car and get something to eat and then get to bed. Isn't that right, Reiko?"

"Yes, Jeff, whatever you say, is good for me."

Eddy slowed down as he took the exit ramp and stopped at the traffic light at the first intersection. Sandor patted Eddy on the shoulder as the van sat at the light. "I'm tired of sitting back here. Let Reiko and me come up front and you get into the back and give me directions from here till where you're taking us."

Eddy turned around to object, but Sandor and Reiko were already getting out of the van. So Eddy got into the back seat while Reiko climbed into the passenger seat and Sandor got behind the wheel. "Okay, the light's changed; which way should I go?"

"Straight, just stay on this road. You won't have to make a turn for a couple of miles."

Now that they were off the highway, the road was unlit and the rain was still pouring down. Sandor turned the windshield wipers to high and put on his brights but it didn't do any good in the fog and he had to lean forward to see down the narrow two lane road. Reiko nervously peered out the window at the limited amount of road they could see before them, "Slow down, it's too hard to see." And when he didn't answer her and maintained his speed, she repeated herself, "Please, you're making me scared!" Sandor took his eyes off the road to glance at Reiko. "Look, don't worry about my driving, okay?"

When Sandor turned back he suddenly saw a tall man with a pale face standing in the middle of the road about 100 feet in front of the on-rushing van. Sandor screamed "Watch out!" and slammed on the brakes and swerved to the right to avoid hitting the man. The van skidded on the wet pavement and went off the side of the road. .

Sandor was jolted by the impact of the steering wheel into his midsection but Reiko and Eddy had been wearing seatbelts and were only shaken. As soon as he saw that Reiko wasn't injured, Sandor jumped out of the van and looked at the front of the van, which had come to a rest near a tree stump. "Damn it! Damn It! The front tire's flat."

By now Eddy and Reiko were standing next to Sandor and looking at the damage to the tire. Eddy grabbed Sandor by the arm and spun him in his direction, "If you'd listened to Reiko and watched how you were driving you wouldn't have lost control of the van! Now look at what you've done."

"Are you crazy? Don't blame me! It was the fault of that guy standing in the middle of the road. He must have been some kind of lunatic!"

"What guy? What are you talking about? There was no one in the road."

"Reiko, you tell Eddy! You saw him back there"

"No, I was watching the road and I saw no one. There was nothing but fog."

"You see, that was it! You didn't see him because of the fog. But I saw him as plain as day. He was standing there and looking at me and smiling. I swear that I saw him. He's back there somewhere. Come on, let's go back and find him."

"What difference does it make at this point? We've got to change that flat tire and get going."

"Yeah, you're right. I'll get the spare out and let's get this fixed. Reiko, why don't you get back in the van and get out of this rain? Eddy and I will take care of this."

As they labored to take off the flat tire and put on the spare, Sandor kept looking over his shoulder, back down the road, through the fog, for a sign of the tall man with the pale face.

As Eddy struggled to keep the jack from slipping on the muddy ground, he didn't know what to make of the story of the mysterious man in the road. But if there actually was a man out there, he wished he could thank him, because fixing this flat tire would give him the extra time he needed so that they wouldn't arrive at the shed by the bridge before Pete and the others got there.

As Reiko sat in the car, in the rain and fog, on a deserted road far from any place she knew, she wished Tommy was with her. And if he had been, he would have told her that there really was a man in the road. And that man was his father.

Pete slowed the van as the road narrowed down to one lane. "Listen to the sound of that water! We must be near the bridge." A few minutes later he stopped the van and pointed out the window. "Look, there's the bridge and the shed, just where the map showed it to be."

Tommy opened his door then asked, "So where are they? Maybe they got here first and they're up ahead."

Pete turned to Tommy. "I don't think so. Josanda Alvarez told me that Eddy was a good man and he'd find a way to stall them until we got here first. He'd never let them get to the Village before we stopped them."

Matt Connors called out from the back seat, "Josanda Alvarez! Just who the hell is that supposed to be? We've driven for all these hours to find my son and now you're talking about someone I've never heard of! Just what does she have to do with any of this?"

"That's nothing you need to know. Just be ready to deal with your son when he gets here."

"And how long are we supposed to wait here before you decide he's already miles ahead of us on the other side of that bridge anyway?"

Reiko's father spoke the one word "Enough!" and then left the van, went over to the bridge and walked across to the other side. He walked back across the bridge and returned to the van. He had to shout to be heard over the roar of the rushing water plummeting down the rapids under the bridge. "The ground is very wet from the rain but there are no tire tracks on the bridge. He has not arrived here yet."

"Good. Then I'm going to block the entrance to the bridge with the van. When they get here they'll have to stop. That's what we want."

Eddy put the flat tire in the back of the van while Sandor spoke to Reiko. "Sorry, that took longer than I thought. The jack kept on slipping in the mud, but now we're ready to hit the road again."

"How much longer? I am so tired from everything that happened today."

"Yeah, Babe, I know how you must feel, and I promise I'm going to make this all up to you. Just give me a chance. Okay?"

Eddy walked back to the front of the van and got into the driver's seat. Sandor turned towards him and barked, "Hey, who said you were driving again?"

"It's pretty tricky driving from here, lots of back roads. It'd be a lot easier to let me do it. Alright?"

"Okay, but let's try to make some time. Reiko's really anxious to get there."

Don't worry, your trip is nearly over." And Eddy pulled the van back onto the road and headed out into the fog.

Twenty minutes later, Sandor was sitting in the back seat and then suddenly called out to Eddy, "What's that noise?"

"It's the rapids. We've got to cross a bridge to get to the cabin. It's really private, just like I told you."

Sandor reached over to Reiko and took her hand. "We're almost there. You'll get a good night's sleep and tomorrow everything will look better. You wait and see."

Reiko gave him a weak smile and withdrew her hand. Though today's journey had seemed to take an eternity, she felt the long road would lead her back to Tommy's arms once again, and she took the sound of the rushing water as a sign that it would happen soon.

Then the van stopped. Sandor spun around towards Eddy. "Are we here? Is this it?"

Eddy pointed out the window. "No, look, there's a van blocking the bridge. I'm going to get out and see what the problem is."

"Okay, Eddy, I'll stay here with Reiko."

As Eddy walked over to the other van, Sandor saw there were four people inside. Eddy started to talk to the driver and then Eddy got into the van and three other men came out of the van and started to walk towards the van he was sitting in with Reiko. As the men got closer he was able to make out that one of the three was about his age and another appeared to be Japanese. As the realization of what this probably meant hit Sandor like a punch in the stomach, Reiko started to scream, "Tommy, Father, it's me! I am here!"

Reiko tried to bolt out of the car but Sandor gripped her by the wrist and with his other hand he leaned forward into the front row and opened the glove compartment and took out the small pistol he had found when he searched Antonio's room. When he had taken it, he had hoped he wouldn't need it, but he wasn't going to let anyone take Reiko away from him, not after all he had been through.

As they approached the van, Pete told Tommy and Reiko's father, "I'll talk to him. You two go around to Reiko's side of the van."

When Pete got to the van he spoke loudly so Sandor could hear him above the rushing water. "You know why we're here. Just let Reiko go and there won't be a problem."

Reiko had reached her free arm through the open window and her father was holding her hand and pressing it to his face. Reiko felt her father's tears on her fingers and cried out to him. He responded by telling her, "It is over now. You will be with us again."

Tommy's heart pounded as he stared at Reiko, but as he was about to pull the door of the van open, he saw the gun in Sandor's hand and he stopped himself. Tommy screamed out, "He's got a gun!"

Reiko's father continued to hold her hand but Pete backed away from the window. "Don't even think about using that gun. You'll make things even worse for yourself."

"I've got the gun, so I'll give the orders. I'm leaving and I'm taking Reiko with me."

Reiko's father heard this and tried to open the van's door but Sandor pointed the gun at him, and the expression on Sandor's face made him back away.

When her father moved away it freed Reiko's hand and she leaned over and used it to scratch Sandor down the length of his face. He shouted in a combination of pain, anger and surprise and without thinking slapped Reiko in the face and knocked her down onto the seat of the van.

Seeing Reiko lying on the seat with a large bruise already blossoming on her face, Sandor was overcome by a tremendous surge of regret. "God, now look at what you made me do. I didn't mean to hurt you."

As Sandor looked down towards Reiko, he heard Pete scream, "Tommy, don't!" and looked up just as Tommy was flinging open the door of the van. Sandor just had time to yell out "Stop!" before Tommy grabbed his arm and tried to wrestle the gun away from him but a shot rang out and Tommy fell backwards through the door of the van and landed in the mud next to the van. Blood from the wound was already soaking his shirt as Reiko screamed his name over and over. Pete ran over to Reiko's father who was kneeling on the floor and holding Tommy's head in his arms. He looked into Tommy's eyes, but all he saw was a vacant stare.

Sandor yelled out the window to Pete, "Don't blame me! He never would've gotten shot if you all just left me and Reiko alone; but now I'm driving out of here with Reiko. And don't try to stop us or I'll use this gun again!" Reiko had collapsed back onto the back seat and lay there sobbing. Sandor moved up to the driver's seat, but when he tried to start the engine he saw that the keys were gone. In an instant he realized that Eddy had taken the keys with him when he left the van.

And then he realized even more. Eddy had fooled him all this time. Eddy had set him up. He must've planned to bring him to this place where the others would be waiting for him. The vein in Sandor's forehead started to throb and he knew there was one thing he had to do before he left here... kill Eddy.

Sandor shouted out the window to Pete, "Hey you, I need the keys to the van. Send Eddy over with them. Do it now, while you've still got the chance!" As Sandor pointed the gun at him and Reiko's father, Pete stood up and ran off in the heavy rain to get Eddy.

Sandor watched as Pete got into the van and Eddy got out and started to walk slowly towards him. But as he came closer, Sandor saw that it wasn't

Eddy who had gotten out of the van, it was someone else. And as he got closer and closer, Sandor couldn't believe what he was seeing. He rubbed his eyes and tried swatting away some of the fog that swirled around the van, but he still saw the same face walking ever closer to him. And he sat there in dazed amazement as his father walked right up to the van and said, "It's good to see you again, son. It's taken me a long time to find you."

"What are *you* doing here? What do you want from me? And why are you trying to help *them*?"

"I'm here to help get you out of this jam. Why don't you just give me that gun before you do something else you'll regret?" And his father held out his hand and waited for Sandor to place the gun in his palm.

Sandor looked at his father's outstretched hand and then up at his face. From the corner of his eye, he saw Reiko's father start to stand up, but he waved the gun in his direction and he sat down again next to Tommy's blood-smeared body.

Sandor turned back towards his father. "So, you've come here to help me, is that it? So, why don't I just give you the gun and you'll make everything alright, is that it? Well, just when the hell have you ever done anything to help me? And I'm supposed to trust you now? I ought to use this gun on you!"

Sandor's father took a step away from the van. "Look, son, I just want to let you know that they're not going to let you leave with the girl. I don't know exactly why, but she's got some special type of significance for them."

"Just cut out that *son* crap! And she's important *to me too* and I'm not leaving here without her. Since they won't give me the keys to this van, I'll have to get them myself. So just start backing up. Me, you and Reiko are going over there together." He turned towards Reiko, who was now sitting up in the rear seat. "Come on, we're going over to the other van. Give me your hand."

"I'm not going anywhere with you!"

"You're making me lose my patience. I've got no time to explain things to you now, but you're going with me."

Reiko didn't move, so Sandor pointed the gun at her father, "Don't force me to do something I don't want to do, Reiko. Just come with me. Now!"

Reluctantly, Reiko got out of the van with Sandor and held his hand as they walked towards the other van. Sandor's father walked ahead of them and kept looking over his shoulder to talk to him. "It's still not too late. They'll let you leave in the van if you just let the girl free. I'll go with you. We'll be hundreds of miles away from here tomorrow. You can get a fresh start. I'll help you, I promise!"

As they walked towards the van, Sandor had to raise his voice as they got closer to the rapids passing under the bridge. "So, it's Reiko *or you*. Tough choice there, *Dad!* I guess I'll have to go with the girl. Isn't that right, Reiko?"

But Reiko wasn't listening. She walked with her face turned towards her father sitting on the ground with Tommy's motionless body cradled in his arms. Her father called out to her, "Do not resist him, Reiko. Be patient. All is not as it seems."

When they reached the van, Sandor pointed the gun at Eddy, who was sitting in the front seat of the van with Pete. "Get out here, Eddy and walk over to the bridge." As Eddy walked the twenty feet to the bridge, Sandor told Pete, "Give me the keys to the van."

By the time Sandor had the keys in his hand, Eddy was at the foot of the one lane bridge. Sandor shouted at him, "I want you to explain this all to me. I want you to tell me you didn't betray me. Go ahead, tell me!"

Eddy stared silently at Sandor and then yelled above the din of the water. "It didn't have to be this way. But when you killed that woman and drugged Reiko we had no choice."

Sandor left Reiko and his father standing by the van and quickly walked towards Eddy. "Of course, you had a choice! You could have helped *me*. But instead you helped Reiko's father and these other people find me. Who *are* they? Why did you do it?"

When Eddy didn't answer him, Sandor raised the gun and pointed it at Eddy's face. Eddy looked back at him. "Go ahead and do it, if that's what you want. This is more important than either one of us. Reiko is the only one who matters."

Sandor started to squeeze his finger around the trigger when he heard a sound behind him and he turned around just as his father was about to tackle him around the waist. The impact sent the gun flying out of Sandor's hand as they went sprawling on the ground.

Sandor and his father grappled with each other as they rolled across the muddy ground. Reiko stood near Eddy, her mouth wide open with a silent scream caught in the back of her throat as she watched them. Pete ran out of the van, but when he moved to intervene, Eddy grabbed his arm. "Let them fight it out between them. Neither one of them is of any use to us anymore." Then, as Eddy reached down and picked up the gun, Sandor and his father struggled to their feet.

With the rapids behind him, Sandor backed away from his father and shook his fist at him. "You've ruined this for me like you've ruined everything else! Now I've got nothing left."

"I didn't want to hurt you but I couldn't stand by and watch you harm any more people. Please come home with me! Your mother lives just to see you again!"

"And that's supposed to make me want to go back with you?"

Matt Connors walked towards his son and stretched out his hand. Sandor looked at him with a sardonic smile on his face and as his father was about to touch his shoulder, Sandor took another step away from him and shouted at Reiko, "I did this all for you, Reiko. I didn't want to hurt anybody; I just wanted you for myself. Nobody's ever going to love you more than me!"

Despite all Sandor had done, when Reiko sensed what was about to happen, a knot formed in the pit of her stomach and she tried to run towards him, but Eddy grabbed her by the arm as she screamed out, "No, don't do it!" And then Sandor abruptly spun around and jumped into the rushing water behind him.

Matt Connors yelled out his son's name, but by then, Sandor's body was bobbing through the water as the current slammed him from rock to rock. As he was swept around a bend, Sandor's body was submerged, with only his arm extending out of the water.

Connors turned towards Eddy and Pete and stared at them with startled eyes and motioned to the water as though he expected them to do something to help, but all Pete could do was stare at the ground. Eddy shrugged his shoulders at him and called out, "It's for the best. He wouldn't let you help him."

Sandor's father turned around again to face the water as it crashed through the rapids. Then he dropped to the ground and held his head in his hands. And so he didn't see Eddy talking into his cell phone. "It's me. It's over! We've got Reiko, but Tommy's been hurt. It may be too late to help him... The other boy? He's gone, drowned in the rapids. His father's still with us. We haven't crossed the bridge yet. Still half an hour away from the Village......Are you sure you want it that way?...Yes, I can understand why....I'll take care of it."

Eddy put away his phone and motioned for Pete to take Reiko back to the van. Then he walked over to Matt Connors, who was still kneeling by the bank of the rapids, and shot him in the back of the head. When Connor's slumped over and lay face first in the mud, Eddy used his foot to nudge the body a few feet until he was able to roll it into the water. The quick current carried Matt Connors' body along, floating face down, as though he was staring into the frigid waters, trying to find the body of his son who had passed this way minutes before.

Eddy watched Matt Connors float downstream for a few seconds, then turned back in time to see Reiko holding Tommy's hand as her father and Pete carried Tommy's body into the van.

Chapter 33

When Eddy got to the van, Tommy was propped up on the back seat with his head resting on Reiko's father, whose shirt was stained with the blood that still seemed to be seeping out of Tommy's body. Pete sat next to him and glared at Eddy, then pointed his finger an inch from his face. "Things weren't supposed to happen this way! When you and Alvarez told me about the Village, about the visions they had for Tommy and Reiko, you didn't tell me Tommy could be in danger. Now look at him! How am I ever going to be able to explain this to his mother? And what about Matt Connors? Where is he? Did you do something to him?"

"No, of course not! But he's not one of *us*. We couldn't let him know where the Village is. Besides, I knew he would want to try to find his son, so I just let him go off by himself."

Pete looked out the window of the van at the barren embankment. "So, where is he now, headed downstream?"

"Yeah, last time I saw him he was moving pretty fast. He must be far downstream by now. But as for Tommy getting hurt, I can't tell you how sorry I…" Eddy's voice trailed off as he looked at Reiko sitting on the floor of the van, tears streaking her face. Eddy was barely able to tolerate seeing Reiko endure such pain. Then he thought of the Village, and the people there who were waiting for Reiko and Tommy to arrive…who had been waiting years for them to arrive. "We still have Reiko to think of and we've got to get her to the Village."

Reiko's father leaned over and stroked her hair, then turned to Pete, "We cannot let the misfortunes of the past prevent us from taking advantage of the opportunities of the future. Reiko's long journey has led her on the path to the Village; we must explore what that destination holds for her. Eddy must take us there now." So Eddy sat down in the driver's seat and started up the van. The wheels spun until they found traction in the mud and then the van lurched forward as it crossed the bridge over the rapids that had swept Sandor and his father away.

They drove for miles through a dense forest on a winding, unpaved one-lane road without seeing another vehicle. Then Eddy suddenly turned the van off the road and drove straight towards a thick grouping of high bushes. Pete nearly bolted out of his seat. "Where the hell? There's no road here. What're you doing?"

Eddy kept on driving straight ahead and as he was about to crash into the bushes, they separated and the van drove through the opening. He drove another hundred yards and then stopped the van in a clearing next to a large group of huts arranged in a circle. Eddy jumped out of the van and motioned for Pete to join him. Dozens of people had left the huts and were moving towards the van to greet them.

Eddy spoke briefly to two husky young men who appeared as if they could fit in seamlessly on the San Jose University campus. They quickly opened the back door of the van and then carefully carried Tommy's body off towards one of the huts. Reiko tried to follow them, but Eddy motioned to her father to keep her near the van.

A beautiful older woman with piercing blue eyes, dressed in flowing white robes with a face suggestive of so many different heritages that Pete could offer no guess as to where she came from, walked up to Eddy and whispered into his ear. Eddy smiled and turned to Reiko and her father. "Very good! We're in luck. Please come with us." They followed the woman to a large hut that was next to the one where Tommy was taken.

Two young men, similar in look to those who had carried Tommy to his room, were standing in the doorway to the large hut. Eddy motioned for them to step aside and before he entered he told Pete to watch Tommy in the other hut. Eddy then walked into the large hut and beckoned Reiko and her father to follow him. It was so dark in the hut that it took Reiko a few seconds for her eyes to adjust, but as she stood there a strong pungent aroma that seemed strangely familiar to her filled the dark room. As more of the hut became visible to her she could see a vase holding cobra lilies sitting on a table near a bed situated only ten feet in front of her. And then she saw two small flashes of light coming from the bed. She took a few steps closer and realized that she was being watched. The glimmers of light were the eyes of someone propped up on the bed. Reiko reached out and grabbed her father's hand and they stood there, neither one wanting to be the one to break the silence in the room.

Eddy walked over and knelt down and kissed the hand of the person on the bed. Reiko heard a few faint words whispered to Eddy. He stood and drew the curtains letting enough light into the room for Reiko to see the person in front of her. And when she finally was able to see him she let out a gasp and took a step backward. It was the ancient man she had seen in a dream while she lay in her bed in the San Jose hospital.

The figure on the bed stared at Reiko. "You shouldn't be so startled, my dear. I think you knew we were fated to meet here." Then he spoke to Eddy in a hushed yet firm, voice. "Bring in the boy." Eddy obsequiously bowed his head. "Of course, Regallus."

Eddy hurried over to the two young men in the doorway and in a few minutes they returned to the hut carrying Tommy's limp body. Reiko gasped when she saw his motionless body and his face drained of all color. As Tommy's body was laid on a cot in the corner of the room, Pete stood in the doorway glaring at the ancient figure on the bed. "Look at what you've done! This never would have happened to Tommy if you and Nurse Alvarez hadn't involved us in all of this!"

.Reiko's father released his grip on her hand and she ran over to the cot that held Tommy. She knelt on the floor and looked at his lifeless body, then turned to her father with a beseeching look on her face.

"It is too late my daughter; even your love may not help him now."

Reiko turned back to look at Tommy again and then she heard Regallus talking to her. "It has been a long journey for you, my child, but our community has waited many years for someone of your abilities to come to us."

"But why have you been waiting? What is it that you expect of me?"

"You possess powers beyond your own understanding. Put your hand on his chest, Reiko. Put your hand on his chest and hold it there for a minute, then tell me what you feel."

Reiko obeyed the command. "I feel nothing. There is no heartbeat. Tommy is gone." Reiko stood and with her face stained with tears, sobbing, she ran out onto the porch of the hut. Staring at the circle of huts that comprised the Village, the tangled events that had brought her to this place flashed through her mind. She thought about the things the old figure on the bed had said about her, and didn't understand what he meant when he talked of the powers she brought with her. But what could thoughts of powers mean to her now, with Tommy's lifeless body lying inside the hut?

And then she felt a comforting hand on her shoulder and as she turned around to accept the embrace of her father, she saw it was actually, impossibly, Tommy who was standing before her. He smiled at her and caressed her face just as she fainted and collapsed into his arms.

Regallus exulted, "She brought him back! Yes, she *is the one.*"

Reiko's father turned to him with an expression of alarm and asked,

"What has just happened here and what do you mean by my Reiko is *the one?*"

"As you can see, my time grows short. For many, many years we have waited for the one who would come and take my place. Our legends told us it would be someone who came to us from very far away. Someone who had escaped death to arrive at our community. Someone who brought powers that would be nurtured and protected here at the Village. My visions had told that the time of arrival was imminent, and when we heard of that horrible bus crash and learned that she was the one who had not only survived, but was able to walk away from it, we knew your daughter was the one we have waited for."

Reiko's father nodded. "Yes, since my Reiko was a small child I have felt that her life has been protected for very special reasons. Two times she should have died and two times she walked away unharmed. But I do not understand this *Village* of yours. Why are you hidden here in the forest? And my daughter is no *legend*. She is flesh and blood, *my* flesh and blood."

"Though your daughter is still yet only a young woman, her bringing that boy back to life has shown our prophesies to be true. I have always been able to alleviate the misfortunes of my followers, but your daughter's gifts far exceed mine. If she can bring the boy back from the *beyond*, then she can do it for all of us."

"No, no, the boy could not have been truly dead. Surely, you cannot believe that she has such a power. Perhaps she is a healer, but no one can reach into the other realm and return the dead back to us!"

"We have spread word of your daughter's arrival and the members of our brotherhood are already journeying here from hundreds of miles away. Tomorrow when we enshrine her as our new High Priestess you will have ample time to see her true abilities displayed."

"High Priestess! How can you talk of such a responsibility? She is just a child!"

"You have been through much today and nothing more is to be gained by continuing this discussion now. Go to sleep tonight knowing that by tomorrow's end you too shall be a believer."

Reiko's father spun around to look at his daughter, but she and Tommy were nowhere to be seen. In their place he saw the woman with the flowing white robes standing on the porch and beckoning to him. He hesitated but felt himself being drawn to her. And then he stared into her glittering blue eyes and he was compelled to follow her as she walked off the porch and into the darkening evening.

She walked across the grounds of the encampment and stopped at a cabin close to the stream that, miles later, would merge with other streams to form the raging waters that had washed Sandor away. Then she entered the cabin, knowing that moments later Reiko's father would be joining her there. And his life, as he understood it, would forever be changed.

At the same time, Eddy stood before Regallus, who was still exalting at Reiko's proof that she was a healer of unparalleled gifts; only darker thoughts were running through Eddy's mind. He had unquestionably served his spiritual master for his entire adult life…but this time an overpowering desire in him gave him the courage to speak his mind. "Regallus forgive me, but I cannot contain my feelings any longer. Why… why Tommy? Why was it so important to bring him here? What role can he possibly play in the future of the Village? I see his presence here as only a risk to us."

"Yes, my boy, I see that what I feared has come to pass. You, yourself have become entranced by the aura of Reiko. But your hopes for a future with her as your mate must be put aside. We must think of the future of the Village…and in my dreams Tommy was protected from death himself to serve a profound purpose…to be the father of her children."

And in another cabin, even closer to the stream, Tommy and Reiko lay together on a huge bed with a large canopy and a headboard encrusted with gold leaf and precious stones. As Reiko slept, exhausted from this tumultuous day, Tommy touched the shredded hole in his shirt where he had been shot. But when he slipped his hand under the shirt, his flesh was completely healed. There was no rational explanation for this and Tommy expected none, for this was only a confirmation of everything he had known all along. He had been protected throughout his life so that one day he would be able to help others in ways that no other could help them. And if his powers did not equal Reiko's, and if his main accomplishment, up to this point, was to help negotiate the events that led to their arriving at the Village, then he still was fulfilled. And looking to the future, he felt his most important role would be to remain at Reiko's side and support her as she became the focal point of this as of yet unknown group of believers.

As all of these thoughts went rushing through his mind, Tommy turned towards Reiko and put his arm over her shoulder as she slept with her back to him. He tried to imagine what the next day would mean for both of them, but decided that wouldn't be any easier to predict than today had been. So he drew himself closer to Reiko and feeling her warm body next to his, pressed his face into her flowing hair and closed his eyes.

But if Tommy could have seen Reiko's face, he would have realized that she wasn't asleep. As she lay there in the dark with Tommy's arm around her, Reiko's eyes were open as confused emotions churned within her; thinking of the man lying next to her who had seemingly returned from the dead because of her touch; could she possibly possess the powers to make such a thing happen? And then she thought of the other man, the one who claimed to have done terrible things all because he loved her too much to lose her… the man who had doomed himself to a watery death because of her.

Chapter 34

He opened his eyes and felt his face pressed into the damp soil. The rapids cascaded past him, spraying his face with a fine mist of cold water. His body felt heavy, too heavy to move, and his head throbbed. In the distance he heard a car pull up and then the engine turned off. A few minutes later he heard the sniffing sounds of the dog as it stopped a few feet from his head and he closed his eyes again. He lay there while the voice of the man called out, "Hey, boy, what'd you find there?"

He heard the squishing sound of the boots coming towards him and then he felt them as the man poked him in the ribs three times. Then the man spoke to the dog again. "When we went huntin' today sure didn't 'xpect to find nothin' like this! Soakin' wet, looks like he just crawled outa the water. Looks like he's dead to the world too. Maybe he's got something we can use."

He felt the man's hands as they tried to squeeze into the back pockets of his pants. "I can't feel nothin' in there. How about I roll 'im over and see what I find." The man shoved at him with his boot but wasn't able to move him, so he bent down and used his hands to roll him over onto his back.

And that's when he reached up, grabbed the man by his shoulders and jerked him down onto the ground. Before the man could scramble to his knees he was smashed in the back of the head with a rock and he collapsed onto the wet ground. Blood started to pour out of his head.

The attack had come so suddenly that the dog hadn't acted, but when he saw the blood covering his master's head he growled, bared his teeth and came at the man who had struck his master. But he'd been alerted by the growl and saw the dog charging him. He stood up and as the dog leapt he caught it by the throat and, in one continuous motion, spun and threw the dog into the rapids passing next to him.

He didn't bother to watch the dog being carried downstream by the swift current, instead he turned back to the unconscious man and pulled off the key chain dangling from his belt and picked up the rifle lying next to him. Then he scampered up the steep incline, found the four wheel drive parked on the side of the road and drove back upstream to look for the bridge where he had jumped into the water.

Tommy was woken by someone he felt gently shaking his shoulder. He opened his eyes to see Josanda Alvarez standing before him in long white robes instead of her usual nurse's uniform. Eddy was standing near Reiko's side of the bed.

Reiko felt the presence of others in the room and sat upright in bed and pulled the covers up to her neck. "Nurse Alvarez, why are you here? How did you know where I was?"

Eddy quietly spoke. "We're all here to help you and to be part of this special day."

"Oh, so now I see! The two of you were working together. When Eddy came to see me in the hospital it was part of your plan. You knew all along that you wanted to bring me to this place. Why did you keep this secret? Why didn't you ask me what *my* wishes were?"

Josanda responded to Reiko's upset. "Yes, Reiko, once they brought you to the hospital and I heard the story about how you survived that accident, I contacted our leader and he told me he had received a vision that you were the one we were waiting for. But please don't make any judgments yet. I have been part of the Village community since my mother brought me here as a child. I know what it has to offer. In time, you will see it was all for the best."

"And by your leader you mean that *old man*? You listen to everything he tells you without question? How can I trust all of you when you have not been honest to me?"

By this time, Tommy was sitting up and listening intently to the conversation.

"Reiko, please, don't speak that way. I know how strange this all seems but I know it's the right place for us to be. It's where our dreams all along have been leading us. Our destiny is to help those who need help the most. With your powers to heal, we can devote our lives to doing that."

Josanda Alvarez reached over and hugged Tommy. "That's right. You've spoken wisely to Reiko. I can see how easy it will be for you to assume a leadership role one day. Your future *does* lie here. A life in our Village; living in the beautiful forest. All your needs provided for by the congregation. Your very presence giving spiritual sustenance and Reiko's healing powers offering the promise of relief from the ravages of the body."

Eddy smiled at Reiko and held out his hand to her. "I just want you to know that I understand how you must feel about the Village. But you can trust me. One day, years from now, you won't even be able to imagine why anyone would want to live anywhere else, in any other way. The outside world will be just a distant memory to you. Now come with me. The ceremony will begin soon and we must prepare you."

When Reiko understood what Eddy was telling her, an overwhelming wave of anxiety washed over her. "Tommy, did you hear what he is telling us? They're never going to let us leave this place!"

From the expression on his face, she realized that Tommy wasn't upset by this. He gave her a beatific smile and said, "Don't worry, Reiko, I'll be here for you. I'll *always* be here for you."

Though Tommy meant his words to be of comfort to Reiko, she heard them as a warning that her destiny was being taken out of her own hands. Then Eddy took Reiko's hand and led her from the hut, as the words "the outside world will be just a distant memory" rang in her ears, and she felt alone, terribly alone.

Reiko's father lay in bed and watched the woman he had met for the first time just yesterday look into a mirror and brush her long dark hair. He thought back to the happenings of yesterday and it all seemed like a long, absurd dream, yet here he was, a sense of shame hanging over him, after sleeping with this woman while his trusting wife waited in Japan to hear word of Reiko.

The woman saw the reflection of Reiko's father watching her and she turned from the mirror, walked back to the bed, sat down on its edge and held his hand. "I have seen the love for your daughter in your eyes. So, I realize that today will either be a glorious one for you...or a most difficult one."

When his expression indicated that he was unaware of her reason for saying this, she continued. "You have a decision you must make. You must stay here with your daughter, or never see her again."

Reiko's father dropped her hand and quickly jumped from the bed. "What do you mean, stay or never see her again? What is about to happen here? Tell me now!"

"I should not have told you even this much, but after what has just happened between us I felt the need to tell you that after tomorrow's ceremony your daughter will spend the rest of her years in this forest."

Pete was woken by the sounds of sawed wood and the hammering of nails. The sun had barely risen, but when he looked out from his hut he saw a party of workers constructing something on a platform in the clearing in the middle of the circle of huts. He tried to walk outside to get a closer look at what was being built, but he was prevented from leaving by a large man with an intimidating attitude standing outside his doorway. So Pete watched from his window until he could see the workers were building two large wooden chairs. And in time he could see that these were no ordinary chairs, for after the ornamentation was added, they were clearly meant to be thrones.

An hour later, the construction had been completed, and Pete was still standing at the window of his hut, watching, as small groups of people entered the Village by foot. Solemn greetings were exchanged among the newly arrived who quickly knelt down on the mats that had been set out in rows facing the thrones. From his vantage point, Pete could see the congregants were of varied ages, but men and women alike all wore the same long flowing white robes that were just short enough to reveal the only differences in their dress; some were wearing sneakers or hiking shoes, while others wore sandals. All were seated silently, facing the platform, an air of expectancy filling the encampment.

But the silence was broken by the sound of a muted horn coming from some unseen location. As the horn played a meditative melody, the kneeling crowd clasped their hands in prayer and bowed their heads. The music grew louder and Pete, a trumpet player himself, couldn't place the horn that could produce that exact quality of sound. Then he finally recognized the instrument from a recording he had once heard of a tribe of coastal Indians. It was no typical horn, but rather a giant seashell. The music swelled as another seashell joined in, and suddenly the melody changed to a triumphant march. The congregants started a chant in a language that Pete couldn't understand, and then got to their feet and lifted their arms and swayed back and forth, their robed bodies billowing like laundry hung up to dry on a windy day.

Then the music abruptly stopped and the crowd dropped back into its kneeling position. Pete leaned out the window of the hut to get a better view of the other huts on the grounds but the guard noticed him and slammed the shutters closed. In a few minutes the silence was shattered by a more fevered chanting and the beating of a loud drum. Pete was compelled to see what was happening, so he charged at the flimsy door of the hut and tore it from its hinges by the impact of his shoulder. He came to a stop on the porch and saw that the man who had been guarding him was now running to join the group of congregants.

Pete cautiously moved towards the chanting crowd but then was stopped in his tracks by the sight before him. An old man wearing garish ceremonial robes was sitting on one of the thrones, waving his arms at the crowd kneeling before him. And sitting on the throne next to him, dressed in a white gown and a veil, Pete recognized Reiko.

After a half hour of driving, Sandor reached the place where he had been separated from Reiko. He slowed the jeep down briefly to cross the bridge, then drove as fast as he could down the unpaved road, hoping it would lead him to Reiko. The ground was still muddy from yesterday's heavy rains and he followed the imprint of tires that had been left by the last car to drive down this road. Sandor didn't know if that was the van that was carrying Reiko, but he had no other leads to go by, so he kept on driving, desperate to see a sign of where she had been taken.

Then Sandor saw the tire tracks swerve off the road towards a cluster of high bushes. He pulled the jeep off onto the grass and got out to look for any indication of why the car had headed in this direction. The grass was matted down where the van had driven over it, but the trail seemed to stop right at the face of the hedge. The bushes were too high for Sandor to see over and too dense for him to see what lay on the other side. He was about to get back in the jeep and try to approach from a different point in the road, when he heard the faint sound of a drum coming from beyond the bushes.

Sandor sensed he would find what he was looking for on the other side of the hedge. He dropped to the ground and started to crawl through the bushes. His face was scratched by the branches growing low to the ground and his shirt was torn as he crawled over a sharp rock. But as he did, the drum got louder and then he heard chanting. He couldn't see her, but he knew Reiko was there. He started to crawl even faster, and the branches cut deeper into him. Blood smeared his face, and he stopped to wipe the blood that trickled into his eyes with the dirt-covered sleeve of his shirt.

He came to the end of the hedge, and when he stood, he faced a circle of huts. In the center of the huts, a hundred feet in front of him, a crowd was kneeling. He saw a number of people in bright costumes standing on a platform, but his eye was drawn to only one person. His lips silently formed the name "Reiko." And in that instant he knew what he had to do, so he crawled back under the hedge, hoping he would find what he needed in the jeep.

As Pete stared in disbelief at the ceremony that had just begun, Tommy ran up to him and grabbed him by the shoulders. The beating of the drums and the chanting had grown so loud that Pete had to stare into Tommy's face to understand what Tommy was yelling at him. He could barely hear Tommy, but he had never seen him like this before. His eyes were blazing with the conviction of a man who knew exactly what course his life must take. "Pete, I can't thank you enough for helping me and Reiko get to the Village, but I'm saying good-bye to you now. You've got to leave before the ceremony goes any further. Only the congregation can witness the crowning."

Pete yelled back at Tommy, "What crowning? What's going to happen?"

"It's Reiko. She'll be the new Priestess of the Village!"

"Priestess! Is that what they're planning to do up on that platform? And what about you? I thought Reiko and you were *together*."

"One day, when Regallus passes from this realm, then perhaps I will be worthy of standing next to Reiko as her co-leader. Until then, I have the comfort of knowing that I have fulfilled the mission my father set out for me, just by bringing Reiko to the Village."

"Tommy, look, I don't know exactly what's going on here, but that Regallus is like some kind of witch doctor to these people. I never would've helped you get here if I knew we were going to land in the middle of some insane cult."

"You're my father's brother, so I'm going to forgive you for saying those things, because if I told Regallus how you felt, he'd never let you leave, or possibly worse."

"Can't you see how crazy you're sounding? They've got you totally indoctrinated. You've got to come with me! It's your only chance. We've got to get Reiko and make a run for it."

"Pete, I'm warning you! If I see that you're still here after the ceremony, I'm not going to be responsible for what happens to you."

"So, are you threatening me now? Is that what you're saying?"

Before Tommy could answer, the drums and the chanting intensified in fervor, and Tommy turned and ran towards the stage, leaving Pete standing in the shadows.

Sandor looked through the back of the jeep and found two road hazard flares, but not the fuel canister he hoped would be there. He stopped for a minute until he decided what to do next. He took off his shirt, ripped it into thin strips and opened the cap to the gas tank of the jeep. One by one, he held the strips of material by one end and shoved the other into the gas tank. When he pulled out the pieces of his shirt, each one was soaked at the end with gasoline. Then he grabbed the flares, and with the other hand holding the strips of material dripping gas, he crawled back under the hedge and headed for the Village.

Reiko's father was standing in back of the chanting crowd, when Pete ran up to him and excitedly pointed towards the platform. "Look at what they are doing to Reiko. Dressed like a bride of that old man. This is insanity. We've got to stop this!"

"Yes, this is far different than I would have imagined it to be. The Village and their leader, no, I was not prepared for this. I had hoped that this would be a place where my daughter and her special abilities belonged, but I fear I have made a tragic mistake."

Suddenly, the drums and chanting stopped. Pete and Reiko's father redirected their focus to the platform. In addition to Regallus and Reiko, Tommy and Eddy and Josanda Alvarez were now standing at the rear of the platform. The crowd was absolutely still, frozen in posture and utterance, waiting to hear the words of their leader.

Regallus walked to the lip of the stage and stretched his arms out to his followers. "The day we have awaited for seemingly an eternity has finally arrived! We have been disappointed by others, but you can place your faith in me today when I tell you that we have been sent a great healer. I have seen her miracles! A spirit more pure than yours, or even mine. Selfless, asking nothing for herself but to have the opportunity to alleviate our suffering. But before I ask you to kneel down and pray to her as you have prayed to me for salvation all these many years, I want you to witness for yourself her great powers."

Regallus walked to the steps at the side of the platform and took the hand of a white haired man who leaned heavily on a cane and led him to the center of the stage. The man dragged his left leg as he walked and when Regallus let go of his hand his left arm hung limply at his side. "Our dear brother suffered a debilitating stroke two years ago and has been offered no hope for recovery. But today his prayers for a return to his former vital self shall be answered. You shall now see for yourself the magic of the healing hands of Reiko!"

Regallus motioned to her and Reiko walked to the center of the stage. She looked back at Tommy for support, but he had his eyes closed and his hands clasped in front of him in silent prayer. She searched for a glimpse of her father but she couldn't find his face in the crowd of people now standing and swaying in front of her, chanting her name over and over. Sweat began to cover her face and the white gown she had been made to wear was sticking to her back. She tried to move closer to the disabled man, but she could not move her legs. Sensing her panic, Regallus put his hand on her shoulder and gently guided her next to the white-haired man, "The time has come, Reiko. Place your hands on our stricken brother!"

Far in the back of the crowd, Reiko's father stared into Pete's face as he pointed towards the platform. "They're all fools! Reiko can't cure that man. He's a stranger to her. They tried to make her into something she is not. Reiko has only been able to help those who she has strong feelings for."

Obeying Regallus' command, Reiko slowly glided her hand over the man's withered arm. She imagined his arm moving freely, possessing all the strength it had before the stroke. Then she knelt down and gently massaged his useless leg, picturing him walking with a full and natural stride. Regallus stood next to her and held up his arms and stretched them towards the heavens. A hush had once again fallen over the crowd. A minute later, Reiko stood up and backed away from the man, spent from the concentrated energy she had expended in her visualizations. Regallus moved behind the white-haired man and put his hands on his shoulders. The air shimmered with the feverish expectations of all those who belonged to the brotherhood of the Village. The man stared at the crowd, his expression betraying nothing. And then he dropped his cane.

Regallus rushed to the front of the stage and held out his hands to the man who stood ten feet away from him. Tommy was now standing next to Reiko with his arm around her, supporting her. The crowd began calling out her name again. The drums pounded out a two- beat cadence that accompanied the chanting of "Rei-ko! Rei-ko!"

Reiko stared at the white-haired man's cane lying on the floor, not knowing herself if she actually had the power to heal this man she had never seen before. She waited for the man to take a step, but then, in the rear of the crowd, an indistinct voice cried out in counterpoint to the chanting of Reiko's name. Then the voices swelled in number and intensity until it became clear what they were calling out …"Fire, Fire!"

Four of the huts were in full blaze, with three others in varying stages of combustion. Clouds of smoke swirled through the air. Eddy screamed out orders and the younger, more physically able members of the brotherhood ran to a shed that contained buckets and shovels. They raced to the few water spigots on the grounds and waited in lines to fill up their buckets and then ran to the closest burning hut. Others were heaping shovelfuls of dirt onto the fires. But by now nearly all of the huts in the Village were threatening to be consumed by the blaze.

Regallus stood on the platform attempting to calm the members of the congregation not involved in trying to put out the fires. But his voice couldn't be heard above the pandemonium that had broken out. Most of the members of the brotherhood had grabbed their belongings and were running towards a clearing in the rear of the Village that would lead them away from the burning buildings.

Regallus dropped to his knees on the stage and began invoking a prayer in hopes of preventing the fire from spreading any further. Josanda Alvarez was kneeling, trying to help the white-haired man who had collapsed onto the platform after the focus had turned away from him. Tommy was tugging on Reiko's arm, trying to get her to leave the platform, but Reiko stood at the front of the stage and searched the chaotic scene for a glimpse of her father among the fleeing crowd.

Pete yelled at Reiko's father, "I'm going up there to get her. And then I'm going to try to get her and Tommy to leave with me."

"No, you must not try this! The flames are not threatening the platform and if you try to leave with her, I do not know what Eddy and his men would do to all of you! We must wait for a better time, later." Reiko's father tried to block Pete's passage to the platform and they grappled with each other briefly, then abruptly stopped when they heard a loud sound coming from behind them.

A jeep had just crashed its way through the high hedge and was picking up speed as it headed straight for the platform. As the jeep swept past Reiko's father he got a fleeting look at the driver. "It is him, returned from the dead!" Pete yelled back, "That bastard, I thought he drowned!"

Seeing Reiko and Tommy standing in the center of the platform, Sandor headed the jeep directly at them. As he did, Tommy dropped Reiko's arm and ran towards the staircase at the side of the stage in an attempt to divert Sandor's attention away from Reiko. Sandor swerved in Tommy's direction and when the jeep hit the platform, the supports holding up that side of the stage were knocked out. Regallus fell to the ground and the rear of the platform collapsed on top of Tommy as he was running down the stairs.

Tommy lay pinned to the ground by the weight of the platform. As Sandor watched from the jeep, Tommy fruitlessly struggled to free himself. He twisted sideways and was able to free his right arm, which he held out towards Reiko. Josanda Alvarez ran over to him, but Tommy was intent on getting Reiko to come to his side. He called out to her, "Reiko, help me! I need you!"

Sandor had backed up the jeep so that it was only a few feet away from Reiko. He leaned out and stretched his left arm towards her. "Reiko, you knew I wouldn't let them take you away. Come with me before it's too late!"

As flames engulfed the huts, Reiko stood on the platform poised on the brink between two men, each beseeching her to come to him. One meant living her entire life in this forest community with a man of deep spiritual commitment to her and the Village; the other, a life with a dangerous, unpredictable man whose love for her wouldn't be denied.

When the jeep crashed into the platform Reiko's father and Pete headed for the platform but before they reached it, they were stopped in their tracks by the sound of gunfire directed at the jeep.

Reiko stood frozen as she watched Eddy holding a pistol and running towards the platform. She knew she couldn't wait any longer to make her decision.

FIVE YEARS LATER

Every morning the six long tables in the community room of the Parish of the Protected Soul, that was perched on the side of a gentle hill overlooking Puget Sound in Washington, were filled with those in need of a breakfast that they weren't able to provide for themselves or their family. The membership of the parish was comprised mainly of the families of low-paid immigrant laborers, single parents, the elderly struggling to get by on a meager pension, and those just plain down on their luck. In return for the meals they received and the care given to their ills, the physically able donated a few hours of their time to working in the food garden that spread out behind the prayer hall. Others were assigned to do pick-ups at the shops in town that supported the parish by donating food. Even the cat that diligently roamed the kitchen storeroom for invading mice was donated by a shopkeeper.

Little Sulli-Ann hoped that her new kitten hadn't gotten lost. She knew it couldn't have roamed far from the little cottage she lived in with her family outside of Mendocino. It was a present from her Grandpa for her fourth birthday and she loved the pretty tawny cat very much. But she couldn't find it anywhere. It wasn't in the house and it wasn't in her mother's flower shop. But then she thought, "Oh, I know where that cat must be!" and so she went off to find it.

Sunday mornings at the parish were always special. After the congregation finished a communal breakfast and the dishes were washed, the tables were moved off to the sides of the room and the benches they had just sat on to eat were set up in rows for the prayer meeting. The men, women and children of the congregation chatted amongst themselves, waiting for the leader of the parish to address them, for this was the main reason they attended on Sundays.

When a member of the parish tried to convince a family member or friend to join the congregation, they usually gave the same reason. "It's our leader; you've got to hear him. It's a hard world out there, you know. And do you know what our leader gives us? He gives us *solace*. Do you know what that means? It's not an easy thing to come by in this world. Why don't you come this Sunday and see for yourself?"

And when they were invariably asked, "Just what is your leader anyway, a priest, or reverend, or pastor, or some kind of guru?" they always gave the same answer.

"No, he doesn't want any titles. He says he's no more important than any of us. We just call him Tommy and that's the way he likes it.

Sulli-Ann didn't always like having a brother and today was one of those days. Sometimes he could be mean and tease her, but even worse was the part about having to share things. Her mother had told her, "Even though there are two of you, your grandfather has given you only one cat to raise. That is because he feels it is very important that you learn how to share responsibilities with each other, especially since you are twins."

So even though today was her brother's day to care for their cat, she missed the kitty and wanted to ask her brother if she could have some play time with it. And she knew that she would probably find her brother, Billy, and the cat, in his favorite place, under the trees down by the pond.

A new attendee at the Sunday morning communal service would usually ask about the small white bungalow just off to the side of the parish hall. "Is that where Tommy lives?"

"Oh, no, that's our clinic. Something's bothering us or one of the kids, well, you know how it is with no medical coverage; we just come over here if it's the usual colds or flu bothering us. And, you know the older folks always got something that needs attention. We all get taken care of real good, and for free too."

"So that Tommy, is he some kind of doctor also?"

"No, he helps out at the clinic, but it's his wife that we go to when we're feeling poorly. Aside from the medicine and herbal cures she hands out, she's got this wonderful touch. If you've got an ache or pain, just five or ten minutes of her massage and you're feeling good as new. And on top of that, she's a beautiful young thing also. That Tommy is a lucky man."

When Sulli-Ann got to the top of the hill that overlooked the pond, she saw her brother and the kitty under the tree and she galloped down the hill to join them.

As she got closer to her brother she slowed down and decided it would be a good time to play a trick on him. So she quietly and slowly sneaked up behind him, and when she was only a few feet from his back she let out a loud "Boo!"

But Billy didn't jump up in surprise. He just sat there holding the cat in his arms. Sulli-Ann shook him by the shoulders and when he turned to face her, she saw that he had a long red scratch mark running across his face. A mixture of blood and tears stained his cheeks.

And then Sulli-Ann saw the cat lying lifeless in Billy's arms. He raised his arms higher to show his sister what he had done. "I didn't mean to do it, I promise! But he kept on scratching my hands, you know the way he does, and I told him to be good, but he didn't listen. And then he gave me this real bad scratch on my face, see here, and I just got so angry. I couldn't help it! I just took him by the neck and squeezed him. I wanted to teach him a lesson, but I musta squeezed too hard. I didn't mean to do it, I didn't!"

Tears formed in Sulli-Ann's eyes, also, as she looked at the body of their cat. But then she heard a voice calling out faintly from up over the top of the hill. It was their father looking for them. "Billy! Sulli-Ann! Where are you? It's time for lunch! We're going to have a picnic! Billy! Sulli-Ann!"

Billy's eyes grew wide with panic. "It's Dad! He's goin' to be angry with me. Real angry! He's goin' to punish me bad. What am I goin' to do? Help me, Annie! You gotta' help me!" Even though they were the same age, Billy always counted on his sister to help him when he had a problem, and he'd never had a problem bigger than this.

Tommy encouraged his wife to close the clinic and join the congregation during the Sunday morning services. The members of the parish were always happy to see her there because it gave them an opportunity to thank her for the good things she had done for them. Over the years, a ritual had evolved, so when she walked into the parish hall on Sundays, Tommy would announce, "Here comes our wonderful angel of mercy!" Then the congregation would rise and applaud her.

She still was embarrassed by this display of appreciation and affection, so as she walked into the hall, all you could see were the brown eyes peering out from over the hand that covered Josanda's blushing face.

Sulli-Ann took the body of the cat into her arms. Its head dangled at a strange angle from its broken neck. Then she heard her father's voice ring out again, this time talking to their mother. "I see them! They're down by the pond. …..Okay, I'll wait for you. We'll go down there together."

Billy squeezed his eyes shut in apprehension. "They're coming, Annie. Please, you gotta help me!" Annie placed the cat down on the ground. Then she gently petted its head and ran her hand down its body, lingering longer to rub the twisted neck.

Coming over the top of the hill, Sulli-Ann's and Billy's mother and father held hands as they slowly walked towards their children. Sulli-Ann's mother stopped and pointed at their daughter kneeling in front of the pond. "Look at her, down there; she's so good with that cat. Look at how it lies still and lets her pet it while it naps. My father would be so happy to see how much they both love their birthday present."

When Sulli-Ann's mother and father got to the big shade tree at the bottom of the hill, they laid down a woolen blanket and took a big bowl of fruit out of the wicker basket that held slices of bread, ham and cheese.

The children were still kneeling near the pond next to the motionless cat, so their mother called to get their attention. "Come on, kids, everybody's hungry. Let's eat!" But when the children turned to come to the picnic blanket, their mother gasped, "Oh, my goodness, Billy what happened to your face?" And their father narrowed his eyes and asked, "It was your cat, wasn't it? You've got to learn to be careful with that thing if you want to keep it." But then he gently touched the scratch on Billy's face and said, "But don't worry son, that scratch isn't as bad as it looks. And after we eat I'll give you a few pointers on how to carry your cat around when it wakes up from its nap."

Later that day, after Reiko and her family had finished their picnic lunch, she leaned against the shade tree and her mind drifted back to the Village... and if she ever wondered whether she had made the right decision that day five years ago, she had only to look at Sandor and Sulli-Ann and Billy playing a quiet game of cards to answer that question; the only disturbance to their peaceful afternoon coming when the cat surprised everybody by jumping into the picnic basket to grab a slice of ham and run off into the tall grass with its prize.